DOCT...
THE I...

DOCTOR WHO
AND THE
LEISURE HIVE

Based on the BBC television serial by David Fisher by
arrangement with the British Broadcasting Corporation

DAVID FISHER

Star

A STAR BOOK

published by
the Paperback Division of
W. H. ALLEN & Co. Ltd

A Target Book
Published in 1982
by the Paperback Division of W. H. Allen & Co. Ltd
A Howard & Wyndham Company
44 Hill Street, London W1X 8LB

First published in Great Britain by
W.H. Allen & Co. Ltd

Made and printed in Great Britain by
Hunt Barnard Printing Ltd, Aylesbury, Bucks.

ISBN 0426 20147 7

1

Brighton

The deckchair attendant shivered in the cold wind off the sea, and cursed for the thousandth time yet another chilly English June. It was going to rain again any minute, he complained to his friend the candy-floss seller. That's all they needed to complete a perfectly miserable day. Anyone with a ha'porth of sense was sure to be in the cinemas or the pubs or the amusement arcades. The beach was deserted. Who'd be fool enough to rent a deckchair in weather like this?

He pulled his coat collar up round his ears, leaned on the iron balustrade of the promenade, and surveyed the row of beach huts.

Then something caught his eye.

That was odd. There was a police box at the end of the row of beach huts. Funny he'd never noticed it before. And he thought he knew Brighton beach like the back of his hand. What was a police box doing on the sand? Didn't make sense. Coppers'd get their feet wet when the tide came in.

In front of the police box he could see a deckchair. Not one of his unfortunately – wrong colour – so perhaps they'd brought it with them. And there was a fellow slumped in the chair, with a brightly coloured beachball and a bucket and space by his side. He was wearing an overcoat, a large hat pulled over his eyes, and a long scarf wrapped round his neck. The deckchair attendant approved. Very sensible way to dress for a day on the beach. That's what made this country great, he thought nostalgically – a steadfast refusal to be deterred by facts. You come to the seaside for the day and, regardless of whether there's six feet of snow along the prom and icebergs are floating down from Hove, regardless of the fact that you're cold, miserable and your boots are beginning to let in water, you come and sit on the beach. Even if it kills you. And with this wind it probably will.

Wait a minute. There was someone else out there. A girl. And what looked like – no, it couldn't be. He could have sworn it was a metal fox terrier. A new breed, perhaps.

Mind you, he said to his friend the candy-floss seller, when you consider miniature dachshunds, I suppose anything's possible.

The Doctor was sulking, Romana decided. He couldn't possibly be asleep – not in this freezing wind. He'd got the co-ordinates of the TARDIS all wrong yet again and just because she had remarked on this – in a perfectly friendly manner – he had gone into a huff. She picked up a stone and threw it violently into the slate-coloured sea.

'There must be somewhere in this whole galaxy,' she remarked to K9, 'where one can enjoy a proper holiday without being frozen to death.'

'There is, mistress.'

'I'm delighted to hear it.'

Taking this as an invitatiion to exercise his memory banks, K9 began to recall the list of recreational facilities available on the galaxy over a period of two or three thousand years.

Romana picked up the beachball and disconsolately began to bounce it.

'Yegros-alpha,' droned K9, approaching the end of

the list. 'Speciality—atavistic therapy of primitive asteroid. Zaakros: galaxy's largest flora collection, including 819 carnivorous species. Zeen-4: historical re-enactments—'

'Re-enactments?'

'You choose what episode in history you want to see re-enacted or take part in yourself. One proviso, however.'

'What?'

'Re-enactment of twentieth century Earth history forbidden: considered to be too violent.'

'Quite right,' said Romana, angrily smacking the beachball, so that it bounced head high. 'That's always the problem with Earth. They never do anything constructive.'

'Sea bathing, mistress.'

'?'

'Traditional Earth exercise when at the seaside.'

'You try it then,' said Romana. She threw the beachball into the sea. 'Fetch.'

The brightly coloured ball bobbed about in the surf about ten yards out. Obedient as ever, K9 trundled down the damp sand and into the water.

There was a loud hiss. A flash. A cloud of blue smoke. And K9 began to sink as seawater seeped through the joins in his metal skin.

'Oh, no! K9!' called Romana. 'I'm coming!' She took off her shoes and plunged into the surf.

The Doctor woke up to discover an indignant Romana, with wet feet and a sorry-looking K9 in her arms, standing over him.

'Look what you've done!' she stormed. 'You've not only got our holiday dates wrong—you've forgotten to update the programme for K9's seawater defences. He's water-logged.'

She shook the dog-shaped computer. The Doctor

could hear water sloshing around inside the metal animal. But he had problems of his own.

'It's the second time I've missed the opening of the Brighton Pavilion,' he complained.

'What are you going to do about K9?' demanded Romana.

'I'll fix him some time.' The Doctor yawned. 'It's this sea air,' he explained apologetically. 'Oh, well, I'll try setting the co-ordinates again.'

He rose to his feet and began to fold up his deckchair.'

'I've got a better idea,' said Romana. 'Before he got soaked K9 gave me a complete list of recreational facilities in this galaxy.'

The Doctor was struggling with the deckchair and didn't reply. He had always liked Earth; it was his favourite planet. But he had to admit that some of their artefacts, like deckchairs and motor mowers and telephones, seemed to be designed with malice aforethought – rather than with the intention of making life easier for everyone. There was, he reflected, a streak of technological sadism amongst Earthlings.

'I like the sound of Argolis.'

'Argolis?' the Doctor muttered indistinctly. He was sucking his finger, having squashed it in the wooden frame of the deckchair.

'First of the Leisure Planets. With a recreational centre called the Leisure Hive. And an Experiential Grid.'

'What's that when it's at home?' enquired the Doctor.

'It offers variable environments designed to stimulate physical, psychic and intellectual regeneration,' explained Romana, parroting K9.

'Sounds like Morecambe on a bad day... Ow!'

8

'Oh, give me that.' Romana put down K9 and disentangled the Doctor from the deckchair, which she then neatly folded up. 'Come on,' she said. 'Argolis next stop.'

She entered the TARDIS followed by the Doctor, grumbling, with K9 tucked under his arm.

The deckchair attendant rubbed his eyes. 'I don't believe it,' he said to his friend the candy-floss seller. 'That police box. It's just vanished.'

'Flaming hooligans,' replied the other gloomily. 'That's who I blame. And comprehensive education. And free school milk. I knew it'd end badly.'

'You don't understand,' protested the deckchair attendant. 'It vanished. Disappeared. Into thin air.'

But the candy-floss seller wasn't listening. He had just spotted a lone Japanese tourist burdened with cameras and three small children and it was a well-known fact in Brighton that the Japanese found candy-floss irresistible.

2

Argolis

Nothing prepared you for the miracle of Argolis. Everyone's first reaction on arriving on the planet was the same – sheer gawping wonder. Even the most experienced space travellers were reduced to open-mouthed bumpkins, unable to believe their eyes.

One of the great hyperspace lines brought you into the orbit of the planet. There you changed to a shuttle in which you descended to the surface. On landing, you pressed the button on the android stewardess, which automatically signed you off the shuttle's passenger log, then you stepped out of the craft onto a moving hover pavement. This carried you gently, silently, up a long tunnel, the walls of which were a uniform dove grey. The tunnel was suffused with a subdued light. The effect was faintly claustrophobic. But not for long. It wasn't enough to cause any distress. At last the pavement deposited you in the first great observation hall of the Leisure Hive.

The contrast with the tunnel was breathtaking. It was like emerging from a womb and stepping onto an immense stage. All around you was glass. You stood inside a huge inverted bowl. Outside you could see the pitted surface of the planet stretching away to the horizon, while overhead arched an immensity of sky. The effect was as if you had been suddenly immersed in a sea of light and colour. Brilliant light. Incredible colour. No rainbows anywhere in the galaxy ever boasted such colours. They flowed over the

10

observation hall in endless, ever-changing waves.

It was only later, when you learned something of the history of the planet, that you realized that the colours which you found so intoxicating were the colours of death...The death of the planet...

Warfare came as naturally as breathing to the Argolin – and about as early in their history. The moment the first hairy, vaguely humanoid creature stood upright on the surface of the planet he grasped in his hand a flint. Before long he discovered how to chip one side of the stone, so that it became as sharp as a razor. Next he tied the flint securely to a heavy stick. Whereupon he promptly struck another Argolin over the head with it.

Thus the first Argolin battleaxe was invented.

Other inventions followed – the spear, the bow, the laser pistol, the intercontinental missile.

Of course not all the other tribes on the planet were equally warlike. Mostly they were quite peaceful. Too busy for war, they occupied themselves inventing such things as the wheel, music, antiseptic surgical techniques, and agriculture.

Since the Argolin were only a small tribe, the others tended to ignore them, or at least keep out of their way if that was possible. And then someone (a non-Argolin) invented a reliable means of transport, and it wasn't. Once the Argolin could move freely about the planet, then, like lice or the common cold, they began to crop up everywhere.

It was therefore only a matter of time before their warriors subdued all the other tribes. Once established as masters of their world, they immediately renamed it – with typical arrogance – after themselves. (Until then it had been known as Xxbrmm after which almost anything was an improvement.) For a century or two the Argolin teetered uneasily on the brink of peace. They were at a loose end: they had killed or enslaved all the other tribes; what else was there left for them to conquer?

Peace was an anathema. Peace was against the Argolin ethos. Peace was bad for you: it made you flabby, weakened your moral fibre, and rotted your teeth. Peace must be avoided at all costs.

The problem was – how? With no one left to fight, what alternative was there?

A group of Argolin elders discussed the matter for a decade or two. Then they came up with a solution which, typical of the race, was both practical and absurd. They evolved a complex and quite useless set of rules and rituals which were intended to govern every aspect of their lives. It was decreed that an Argolin should wear certain colours on a particular day, eat certain foods, wash himself or herself in a particular manner, wear certain insignias, and so on. Their entire life was to be devoted to keeping up with those ever-changing rituals. Failure to observe them, no matter how ludicrous they might be, came to be regarded as an insult by another Argolin. Insults could only be exculpated through mortal combat, which was conducted under another set of complex rituals.

The tournament and the duel therefore became a substitute for war. Indeed, it became a way of life, or death, for every adult Argolin. They killed each other with an enthusiasm and determination the subject races could only applaud.

At the height of what came to be called the Golden Age of Heroic Combat most male Argolin had at least a dozen duels pending, not to mention various courtly tournaments at which they were expected to shed blood, their own, or someone else's. Female Argolin were not forgotten either. Once past childbearing age, they were required to avenge the slights and insults accumulated over twenty years. A woman could inherit a backlog of a hundred or more unfought duels, and she was expected to devote her declining years to fighting them. Those elderly females who survived tended to be scarred veterans of numberless combats, and were used to frighten Argolin children instead of the traditional bogeyman.

The principles of chivalry and the exploits of Argolin heroes were celebrated in a thousand ballads and verse sagas, with which Argolin knights were wont to regale themselves whilst recovering from wounds, or merely resting between tournaments.

The Saga of Herell the Hapless and Mako the Mighty was typical of the genre. Herell, a young knight newly initiated into the rituals of chivalry, was challenged to a duel by Mako, a one-legged giant. He had lost his leg several years before in a previous duel. Herell decided the odds were unfair. Not only was Mako ten years his senior, but since the chosen weapons were to be huge two-handed swords, Mako's lack of mobility placed him at an immediate disadvantage.

Only the most agile could hope to succeed with such weapons. Before the moment of combat Herell therefore hewed off his own left leg and, sword in both hands, hopped painfully towards his opponent. When Mako's squire pointed out that his master was minus a *right* leg and the advantage was still not equally balanced, Herell angrily struck off his other leg and prepared to fight on two bloody stumps. Mako, not to be outdone, cut off his own left leg. Both combatants died of shock and loss of blood without striking a blow at each other.

This was regarded as one of the most glorious

moments of Argolin chivalry.

Just when it seemed possible that the Argolin might – unaided – wipe themselves off the face of the planet, someone (a non-Argolin) discovered the means of interplanetary flight. The surviving Argolin could breathe again. At last they could devote themselves to conquest. They stopped killing each other and occupied themselves with killing the inhabitants of other planets – according to the strictest rules of Argolin chivalry, of course.

Their conquests continued until they came across a race as warlike as their own.

The Foamasi were green and scaly, reptilian in appearance, vaguely resembling man-sized lizards. Like the Argolin, they too dominated their environment by sheer aggressiveness. Unlike the Argolin, however, they did not develop into a knightly, aristocratic society. Cold-blooded, more numerous than the humanoids, the individual in Foamasi society was less important than the clan, the extended family. It was the clan against the world. One family pitted its wits and its members against another, winner take all, no quarter given or asked.

The only rules were those of the jungle. Kill or be killed; eat or wind up as the shish kebab. Every Foamasi enjoyed complete existential freedom of action. Nothing was forbidden: no act of violence was too extreme. He could do anything he liked to anyone else, just as long as they were not members of his own extended family. The family was sacred. For good reason; they were often your only protection against other Foamasi.

The consequence of this was that no Foamasi ever dined with a non-member of his family unless he carried with him the full range of poison antidotes in the pharmocopoeia and wore a suit of titanium alloy

14

chain mail, guaranteed proof against any weapon or projectile short of an artillery shell.

In place of the Argolin knight, that faintly ludicrous figure *sans peur sans reproche,* the Foamasi found their folk heroes amongst professional hit men: assassins. The poisoner, the strangler, the wielder of the fastest electric stiletto, were celebrated in song and story.

Since they were an intensely competitive race by nature, it is not perhaps surprising that the Foamasi formalized their natural predeliction for sudden death. Murder came to be regarded not only as one of the fine arts, along with water sculpture and aural architecture, but also the sport of kings and the entertainment of the crowd. Television helped. The big festivals were televised. Even minor inter-family competitions were followed with avid interest. Inevitably wagers were made on the result, and before long several Foamasi clans moved in and organized gambling on a planetary scale. Thus began a division of the race into two different branches, the punters and the bookies, those who bet and those who organized the betting: what came to be called the White and Black Foamasi — although this had nothing whatsoever to do with scale colour, since all Foamasi were uniformly green.

Sharing one galaxy, it was only a matter of time before the Argolin and the Foamasi met. And once that occurred it took them precisely six minutes to become locked in pointless, hopeless combat.

The excuse for the war — not that either side really needed one — was a minor asteroid which lay roughly half-way between Argolin and Foamasi territory. This chunk of space dirt held together by frozen methane was only thirty kilometres in diameter, and known to be useless as an outpost and valueless as a

15

source of mineral wealth. Nonetheless both sides laid claim to it.

The Argolin sent a ship to establish a garrison on the place. So did the Foamasi. The two ships met on collision course in orbit around the asteroid. The Argolin commander demanded that the Foamasi vessel change course. The Foamasi captain insisted that if anyone was to change course it must be the Argolin. Before the question could be resolved one way or the other the two ships struck head on. The resulting fireball melted the frozen methane and vaporised several kilotons of space debris and destroyed the asteroid. It also caused a war.

It must be admitted that the war between Argolis and Foamas was not the most destructive on record. On a scale of 1 to 12 according to the Shebunken Formula, which was devised by Prof. Igor Shebunken of the University of New Caledonia to measure the destructiveness of international or interplanetary conflict, the Argolin-Foamasi War scored a mere 10·3, somewhere below total destruction and above the semi-genocidal level.

Seventeen hundred and sixty-two Argolin struck the planet of Foamas, reducing it to a burned crisp. A red-hot cinder incapable of supporting even calorific bacteria. The two thousand or so Foamasi missiles which struck Argolis didn't have quite the same effect. True, the missiles burned off the surface of the planet and hurled the debris into the stratosphere. There, owing to gravitational forces, the dust remained. Ultra-violet light from Argolis' four suns turned the dust into a veritable symphony of colour.

A million rainbows, perpetually shifting, forming and re-forming, glowed with jewelled splendour over the desert that was now the planet Argolis.

The Argolin, those who survived, were not slow to

take advantage of this. They turned Argolis into the first of the Leisure Planets.

The time was ripe for such developments.

Thanks to the technological revolution of seventy-five years before, which had freed the inhabitants of three-quarters of the galaxy from the necessity of work, time began to hang heavy on everyone's hands (or whatever limbs they were blessed with). War and crime seemed to provide the most popular alternative to the agony of boredom. Then, just when it seemed that the whole galaxy would descend into barbarism, Hyperion C. Blackadder, an Irish missile research engineer working on Tethys, stumbled across the principle of hyperspace drive. (Literally stumbled across it, in fact. He found himself on Io before he realized what had happened, and spent the next four years trying to return to Tethys.) Blackadder's discovery revolutionized intergalactic travel. It brought the farthest reaches of the galaxy within only a few days' travelling time. You could travel from Odin-3 to Xeros-9 in under a week.

Once it was discovered that there were few technical limits to the size of vessels that could operate in hyperspace, the entrepreneurs moved in. Intergalactic travel was soon open to every sensate being with enough interplanetary credits to purchase a ticket. And so creatures from over forty different star systems went traipsing around the galaxy in search of recreation, good weather, and a really cheap holiday.

Many of them went to Argolis.

Because Argolis was special.

From inside the safety of the great glass Leisure Hive the planet was a wonder to behold. Visitors never tired of sitting and watching the incredible ever-changing colours. It was as if nature had become a painter and Argolis her canvas.

17

But it was a deceptive beauty. A dangerous beauty. The picture had to be kept behind glass. Because the atmosphere of the planet was poisonous to most forms of life in the galaxy. Almost nothing could breathe the air of Argolis and survive. You could look; you could admire; but you couldn't walk the sands of Argolis and draw in deep lungfuls of Argolin air.

When the tourists grew bored with the ever-changing colours, there was always the Experiential Grid to entertain them – that masterpiece of Argolin technology, the climax of a century of study of a theoretical sub-atomic particle, the tachyon.

The irony of it was that in order to survive, the aristocratic knights of Argolis, once the scourge of the galaxy, were now reduced to becoming tourist guides to their own destroyed planet – a job they performed with cheerless efficiency.

3

Brock

The figure in the holograph was soberly suited and wore an air of restrained gloom, like a high-class mortician. He was, in fact, the Terran business adviser to Argolin Leisure Enterprises Inc. which, like so many galactic commercial operations, was now registered for tax purposes on Terra.

Over the years Earth had transformed itself from a polluted, dying world into a tax haven. (The Cayman Islands of the Galaxy, as one wag put it.) Its population, reduced by a series of wars to under twenty million souls, had all become accountants or service engineers for the tea-dispensing machines which proliferated in Terran offices.

Augustus Brock spoke into the hyperspatial desk communicator in his office in New Delphi. His holographic image was projected into the Council Chamber of Argolis ninety-three light years away – with only a slight time lag caused by the inevitable hyperspace distortion.

Brock was one of Terra's top accountants. As such he was used to rapt attention if not instant comprehension, as he picked over the entrails of some commercial enterprise. He was not encouraging about Argolis.

'I must tell you that all our predictions, even those based on optimum exploitation of existing facilities, indicate a probable financial down-run.'

The four Argolin remained impassive. Not by the

slightest change of expression, not by the flicker of an emotion, did they reveal that they hadn't the faintest idea what the accountant was talking about.

'And that,' went on the Terran, encouraged, 'is the optimistic scenario.'

Pangol, the youngest member of the Argolin Council, glanced at his fellow members with some irritation. You could take Argolin impassivity too far, he thought. 'What's that mean in plain language?' he demanded.

'Bankruptcy.' The Terran turned away and played a brief arpeggio on the keyboard of his computer. He checked the computer display and shook his head sorrowfully. 'Indeed I will go further,' he said. 'Projection-wise, based on thirty different economic scenarios provided by our business augury department – total bankruptcy.'

No one spoke.

Once again Brock looked round the Argolin Council, wondering if anyone had taken in what he had said. He decided to repeat his prophecy: 'Total bankruptcy.'

Morix, the senior member of the Council, spoke gently as if explaining simple facts to a child. 'We've always known the Leisure Hive was expensive to maintain,' he said. 'And it's true that last year's bookings were down—'

'They're even worse this year!'

'—but surely in the long run—'

'There won't be any long run,' said Brock. 'Don't you understand?' He took a deep breath and plunged on. 'Shielding the Hive from radiation alone eats up 61·5 per cent of your income, even when you're booked solid the whole year round. And for the past two years the Hive has been less than fully booked, even in the high season. How much longer do you think you will be able to preserve the integrity of the Hive? If the technical reports are to be believed, some of the shielding is already due for replacement.'

'What about next year's bookings?'

'They could be mildly described as disastrous. They will amount to thirty per cent or less of this year's bookings.'

Pangol stirred angrily in his chair. 'You are our booking agent as well as our accountant,' he snapped. 'Bookings are your responsibility. If you are not up to the task, we can always find ourselves another agent.'

Morix laid his hand on the young man's arm. 'Calmly,' he admonished. 'With dignity. Remember, we are Argolin.'

'Dignity!' cried Pangol. 'It is the Argolin disease. We need more than dignity in order to survive in the world.'

But Brock, who privately agreed with the young Argolin, refused to be deflected from his argument. 'The facts,' he said, making a steeple of his fingers, 'do not suggest that any change of booking agency, advertising policy, or even accountant will affect the trend.'

'I do not understand what has gone wrong,' complained Morix. 'After all we were the first in the field of Leisure Planets.'

'Precisely,' agreed Brock. 'The glorious past is, I regret to say, as is so often the case, past. Argolis is simply out of date. Other Leisure Planets have moved with the times. They are constantly looking for new pleasures and delights for their visitors.'

One by one he ticked them off on his fingers. 'Non-gravity swimming pools. You can dive upwards or downwards into or out of the pool. Then there are robotic gladiatorial games. Psychic gymnasia.

'Look,' he went on, 'it's your planet. Make it more attractive to visitors and they will flock here in their thousands – and keep coming back.'

'Easier said than done,' observed Morix.

He thought it ironic that the Argolin found it easier to conquer a galaxy than to run a successful Leisure Planet. The practice of warfare demanded a combination of skill and simple virtues ideally suited to the Argolin temperament, whereas the management of people's leisure pursuits required the adaptability of Robinson Crusoe combined with the diplomatic skills of Machiavelli. As he was forced to admit to himself, the knights of Argolis were totally unsuited to commerce.

'What other Leisure Planet has pioneered a whole new science?' demanded Pangol.

'I suppose you're referring to tachyonics,' replied Brock. 'If you will remember, each year I have pointed out to the Board that you simply cannot continue to invest vast sums in research. The tachyon is a scientific curiosity, nothing more.'

Pangol clenched his fists. The tachyon represented the Argolin holy of holies, the one intellectual frontier they had made their own.

It was of course typical of the Argolin that they should have embraced something as abstruse as the tachyon – which is a hypothetical particle first propounded by Terran physicists in the twentieth century. Einstein's special theory of relativity led many of them to the view that there was a yet undiscovered particle possessed of the most extraordinary properties. This particle, they theorised, only came into existence when it was already travelling faster than the speed of light. On the face of it this seemed to make nonsense of Einstein's own theory, which proposed the velocity of light as a constant. But the physicists suggested an ingenious solution to the problem.

One of the curious properties of this particle, they claimed, was that two tachyons would be able to occupy the same space at the same moment in time — with only the minimum of elbow-rubbing and general bad temper. Normally in the world of physics such behaviour would result in a massive explosion. It didn't in the case of the tachyon because the particle possessed either imaginary momentum and energy or else imaginary mass. No one was quite sure which, because no one had ever succeeded in isolating a tachyon and subjecting it to any tests.

At least no one had done so until the Kromads, a nocturnal feathered race with an interest in the vaguer reaches of theoretical physics, finally cornered the bashful tachyon. In an experiment of remarkable elegance they fractionally slowed up a number of the particles which then collided — and blew up their sun. After which disaster no one, except the Argolin, was prepared to mess around with tachyonics any more.

'Perhaps if there was a programme of investment in the Leisure Hive?' suggested Morix.

Brock shook his head. 'Where would you get the money?' he demanded.

'There are bankers on Ygros-10,' said Morix with obvious distaste. The aristocratic Argolin had always despised those who dealt in mere money. 'You yourself represent various investment groups.'

Brock sighed. 'Tell me,' he asked, 'how can I possibly recommend to any banker or any of my clients that they should invest in a decaying enterprise which is on its last legs?'

But Pangol had heard enough. The Terran upstart had dared to cast aspersions on the glory of Argolis. Angrily he crossed the room and turned off the hologram. Suddenly in mid sentence the figure of the Terran accountant faded from view.

The other Argolin smiled approvingly at each other. There was a time, not too long ago, when at the slightest sign of contempt on the part of any foreigner, Terran or whoever, they could have spitted the offending churl on the end of their electronic lances. But these days were gone, more's the pity.

Morix shook his head. 'That was discourteous, Pangol,' he protested. 'There must be no more aggression on Argolis.'

He glanced uneasily up at an ancient helmet that hung on the wall...an ancient Argolin tournament helmet and a lasting symbol of the ferocious Argolin past. It was the Helmet of Theron, the helmet which the captain of the first great Argolin expedition to the stars had worn in some of his most famous battles. Morix feared the Argolin past. It had brought his people to the very edge of destruction. It might destroy them yet.

He looked sadly at Pangol. There the old Argolin spirit still burned fiercely.

There was nothing more boring, thought the young visi-journalist, than waiting in Old Delphi galacto-port for something to happen. Some story to break. Anything. It didn't matter what. Just so long as it was newsworthy. All it needed was some celebrity to breeze through on his, her or its way to — where? That was the trouble. No celebrity ever visited Terra any more.

'That's the problem with Earth these days,' his companion, the oldest visi-journalist on Terran duty, observed with a yawn. 'Nothing ever happens here. Earth's become the Switzerland of the galaxy. A journalistic dead end. The elephants' graveyard. The place where they send old visi-journalists to die.'

24

The younger man yawned too. He had heard it all before: yesterday to be precise and no doubt he would hear it again tomorrow. The old visi-journalist was nothing if not predictable. Hence no doubt his appointment to Terra, after a lifetime spent covering non-stories in every crummy planet in the galaxy.

'Has it ever occurred to you,' asked the young journalist, 'that we may actually be seeing news stories all around us? Here and now. And we can't recognize them because we've lost the talent to see news when it happens.

'Take her,' he went on, pointing to one of the passengers who had just entered the departure lounge.

The passenger in question was a woman, beautiful, elegant, wearing flowing orange robes and an extraordinary coiffeur. Her hair was piled up on her head in a smooth cone and glittered with jewels. She carried a small black globe which was attached to her wrist by a silver chain.

'You don't see many Argolin here, do you? Not surprising really. There can't be that many of them left.'

The older journalist didn't answer. His almost atrophied news sense was beginning to twitch like a sleeping spaniel.

'I wonder who she is.'

'Mena. The Consort of the Heresiarch of Argolis.'

'I went to Argolis once when I was a kid. First of the Leisure Planets. Very colourful as I recall—'

But the old journalist was no longer listening. He had gone over to speak to his friend who was a booking clerk. The young journalist joined him.

'She arrived here about three weeks ago,' the booking clerk was saying.

'One of your regulars?'

'Never seen her before,' replied the clerk.

25

'Who's the fellow with her?' asked the young journalist.

They turned and looked at the Terran who was seeing her off.

'Name of Hardin,' said the clerk, checking his booking list. 'He's booked on the next flight.'

'To Argolis?'

The clerk nodded.

'Wonder why he's not travelling with her,' remarked the young journalist.

His colleague was trying to place the Terran. He had seen him somewhere before. Then it came to him: 'Particle engineer. Spoke at a scientific congress I covered about two years ago. Gave a paper on – what the devil was it now? – "Environmental Instability: the Problems of Tachyon Technology".'

'The things you remember,' said the young journalist with a laugh. 'I've never met anyone with a brain packed with so much useless information. Tachyon technology, indeed: that's hardly galaxy-shattering news. No wonder the network posted you to Terra if that was your idea of a scoop.'

But the spaniel refused to lie down.

'Why aren't they travelling together?' demanded the old journalist. 'Something odd there.'

'Maybe she doesn't want to listen to any more boring old lectures on Environmental Instability or whatever it was during her trip home.'

The old journalist acknowledged the justice of the remark. It hadn't been exactly a scintillating conference, he recalled. Even amidst a desert of technical gobbledegook the lecture in question had seemed particularly opaque. He remembered that the network had not used one of the stories he had filed from the conference. When *had* they last used one of his stories?

'What do you think?' he asked the booking clerk.

'The chap's probably just off to Argolis to fix their tachyon generator,' replied the latter. 'You know what the Argolin are like. Proud as princes. They wouldn't want to travel with the hired help.'

The spaniel gave a last twitch and went back to sleep: the old journalist shrugged. Oh, well, he thought, it was probably nothing.

Just then a silver box the size of a packing case complete with an array of sensors entered the departure lounge. It hovered an inch or two off the floor and moved purposefully in the direction of the Extra-Terrestrial Travellers' Bar. The case was a mobile environment, provided by the hyperspace lines for use by creatures for whom Terra's atmosphere was poisonous. The box could be steered by its occupant and a variety of translating devices enabled the traveller to communicate his, her or its wishes in any hyperspace port of the galaxy.

'Know who that is?' demanded the young journalist, gathering his mini-cam and recording and translating gear.

The old journalist shook his head. He found it increasingly difficult to keep track of Off-World celebrities.

'One of the mud dancers from Hesperus-2. They came sixth in the last intergalactic final. Come on,' he said. 'Ought to be a story there.'

But there wasn't. At least the network didn't think so.

Later, over a glass of synthetic Scotch, the older journalist remembered why he had been curious about the particle engineer and the Argolin woman. After all, why should the Argolin need an expert on environmental instability when, as everyone knew, they had a perfectly good tachyon generator?

4

The Generator

That morning in his bare, cell-like room Morix, Heresiarch of Argolis, had had his first seizure. A fit of coughing that left him grey and gasping for breath. He realized the significance of the attack. He had even been half expecting it. Now it had come he would face death quietly and with dignity, like a true Argolin knight. But first there were duties still to perform.

Too weak to stand, he summoned the medical guides to bring a hover litter. The two orderlies laid him on the litter and bore him to the boardroom where they sat him in his chair.

At his command they pressed a button on the desk console. A blank area of the boardroom wall slid back to reveal a view of the Argolin landscape. Not the landscape as it was today – cold, jewelled, glittering, lit by the refracted colours of a million rainbows. But the landscape of Argolis as it had been before the Foamasi War. The land was green and lush, with rolling hills and dense woods where once Argolin knights had hunted. Flowers grew in profusion. There was an abundance of fruit. The air was perfumed and sweet.

Pangol entered the room, but Morix did not hear him. He was lost in contemplation of the past beauty of the planet.

Morix's breath rattled in his throat. 'There must have been a great madness in our race,' he whispered, 'to have allowed all this to be destroyed.'

Pangol was not impressed. 'The Foamasi struck when we were not prepared,' he said.

'We both struck together,' declared Morix. 'I should know, I commanded one of the great hyperspace war galleys. I remember I was astonished to discover a race that reacted in battle as swiftly as the Argolin. I had barely ordered the crew of my war galley to fire the missiles, when I heard, over the hyperspace link-up, a Foamasi captain give the identical command.'

Morix shook his head. 'No,' he said. 'We were both equally guilty.'

Another fit of coughing overtook him. He lay helpless in his chair, unable to move. One of the orderlies wiped his brow. Morix nodded his thanks. He seemed to be ageing before their eyes.

The screen on the desk console flickered into life, revealing the face of the guide who was in charge of welcoming the shuttle arrivals.

'Heresiarch, a Terran has just arrived off the shuttle and begs audience—'

'I don't beg a damn thing!' snapped a familiar Terran voice. 'I just want to see Morix. Tell the Chairman of this Leisure Planet that it's urgent. I've no time to waste on Argolin ceremony.'

'His name is Brock,' explained the guide.

Pangol reacted angrily to the name. 'Come to sneer at us no doubt,' he said. 'There was a time when a mere Terran would have been flogged for such temerity.'

Morix silenced the younger man with a feeble motion of his hand. 'Send him to me,' he whispered.

Pangol gazed fondly at the ancient duelling helmet that hung on the wall. The Helmet of Theron the Great. If Theron had only discovered Terra on his first space voyage, he thought, he would have left that miserable planet and everyone on it barbecued to a crisp. Then there would have been no Brock to insult the Argolin now.

Morix motioned to the orderlies to press the button that controlled the wall panel. He watched the ancient landscape of Argolis vanish behind the white section of wall.

Brock threw open the door and burst into the room. He was a thick-set, dark-haired man who burned with a restless energy the others could feel. It was like standing close to a noisy engine: you felt the valve settings needed adjustment. He was accompanied by a gaunt Terran who carried a briefcase and offered nothing by way of greeting.

'Mr Chairman,' said Brock genially, 'and my dear Pangol, after all these years of dealing with you via the telecommunicator, here I am at last in the all-too-solid flesh.' He patted his slight paunch and laughed. He slapped Pangol on the shoulder and then lumbered over to shake Morix by the hand. He stopped in his tracks, aghast at the sight of the figure in the chair. Could this grey, waxen, shrunken creature be Morix, last of the Heresiarchs, Chairman of the Leisure Planet Argolis Inc.?

'Morix?' he asked questioningly.

With agonizing slowness the figure inclined his head.

Brock turned to Pangol for explanation. The latter replied bitterly: 'Hard to recognize, isn't he?'

'Well, I—' The Terran spread his hands, lost for a moment for words. 'What's the matter with him? Is he ill? Is there anything I can do?'

'He's dying,' said Pangol brutally. 'Take a good look. Outsiders never get the chance to see it. It's our secret. The way the Argolin die. The way we all die on this planet.'

'I don't understand.'

'It's because of the Foamasi,' explained Pangol. 'The radiation from their missiles affected our metabolic rate, slowing it for long periods of time. For years we don't appear to age at all. It's as if we were kept under glass. The radiation actually preserves our bodies – until what we call the Twilight Time.' Pangol grinned wolfishly. 'Then suddenly some metabolic key is tripped – and the whole ageing process begins. It speeds up. In a few hours, a few days at most, our bodies age fifty or sixty years. An Argolin can be fit and well one minute, and the next he has become a shell, a skeleton ravaged by the years.'

With a great effort Morix spoke: 'Forgive Pangol, my dear Brock. He knows I have only a little time to live. He is angry. But there is no reason to be. Death, when it comes to the Argolin, strikes swiftly.'

Brock shook his head. 'I didn't know,' he said.

'No one knows,' snapped Pangol. 'We don't broadcast the fact. Long ago the Argolin Council decided to keep it a secret. They decided it might be bad for the Leisure Planet business. Might put the holiday makers off if they knew that their charming guides carried a biological time bomb around inside them.'

'If I had known, I would never have come—' Brock glanced uneasily at Klout, his lawyer.

'Why did you come here?' asked Morix. 'In the past we've always conducted our business by tele-communicator. And why bring a lawyer with you?'

He glanced suspiciously at the gaunt silent figure who stood beside the accountant.

'Because I thought we might need one.'

'Why?'

Brock sighed. It was going to be hard; harder than

31

he had thought. 'Since I spoke to you, there has been an offer,' he said.

'An offer? From whom?'

'From a group with 30 trillion galactic credits to invest.'

A rare smile lit up Morix's drawn features. 'They want to invest in the Leisure Hive?' he asked.

Brock shook his head. 'Not exactly, Mr Chairman,' he said. 'They want to buy Argolis. The whole planet. Lock, stock and radioactive barrel.'

The silence which greeted his words seemed to Brock to hang in the air of the boardroom, like some bird of ill omen. He coughed. 'I think it's a very generous offer,' he said at last.

No one replied.

He said: 'I don't think we're likely to get a better one.'

'Buy Argolis?' Morix repeated blankly.

Brock hastened on. 'That's why I thought I ought to come and see you in person,' he explained. 'In view of the financial state of Argolis Leisure Planet Inc., believe me it's an offer you cannot afford to refuse.

'Just think of it,' he continued, emboldened. 'You can unload this white elephant of a place and buy yourselves another planet. There are plenty for sale in this quadrant of the galaxy. You can have a choice of atmospheres. Oxygen. Nitrogen. Methane. Argon. Whatever suits you: just take your pick.'

Still no one replied.

'Don't think of it as losing your home,' he advised. 'Remember you'll be able to take your people from this dead, poisoned world to a new planet where you can actually walk around on the surface and breathe the air. Or methane. Or argon. Whichever takes your fancy....'

His voice died away.

Brock swallowed.

Pangol could contain himself no longer. 'We will not sell our birthright!' he cried. 'Argolis is not for sale!'

After a glance at Morix, who seemed to have fallen into a coma, Brock turned on Pangol. He had taken quite enough from this young Argolin. It was time to acquaint him with the brutal facts of commercial life. 'That, my dear Pangol, is not for you to decide. Nor for Morix, come to that. It is a board decision. The board of Argolis Leisure Planet Inc. will be the final arbiter.'

'I wouldn't bank on that,' replied Pangol. 'The Argolin always obey their leader.'

Silent, immobile, K9 stood forlornly on a table while the Doctor unscrewed his side panel. As soon as he began to ease the panel off, about half a gallon of cold seawater gushed out all over his feet.

'Urgh!' cried the Doctor, hopping up and down.

Romana, who was adjusting the controls on the console in preparation for landing, ignored him.

Grumbling to himself, the Doctor stood on one leg and removed a shoe, which he then emptied of water.

'I'll squelch for the rest of the day,' he complained. 'Probably go down with 'flu or pneumonia.'

There was a faint jarring as the TARDIS alighted.

'We've arrived,' announced Romana.

'Oh,' said the Doctor, studying the jumble of wet and tangled relays and micro circuits which filled most of K9's interior. 'It'll take ages to get him operational again.'

Romana prepared to leave the TARDIS. 'Well, I'm starting my holiday now,' she said, pressing the lever on the console which activated the doors. She stepped out into the Great Leisure Hall of Argolis.

Unhappily the Doctor picked a piece of seaweed off K9's motor circuits. Then a thought occurred to him. 'We're hardly likely to need K9 here, are we?' he said.

He was never more wrong.

Romana was standing in the middle of the Great Hall. She was staring upwards, lost in wonder as the myriad colours of Argolis chased each other in countless different shades and patterns across the sky.

No one had noticed the arrival of the TARDIS, largely because everyone else, like Romana, was goggle-eyed at the view. As for the police box itself, it fitted in amongst the many kiosks and cabins in the Great Hall. In any case those visitors who were not busy gawping at the Argolin rainbows were watching the big bubble screen set above a kind of booth.

The Doctor locked the TARDIS behind him and moved over to the screen. On it, in 3-D, he saw that a game of squash was in progress. The two players, both humanoid, were very expert. The ball flashed back and forth with monotonous regularity. Then something strange happened to the game. The ball assumed a life of its own. The laws of gravity ceased to apply. The players were now seen to be in a state of free fall, yet they still continued to stroke the ball back and forth.

'Clever,' observed Romana, who had come up to stand beside the Doctor. 'Wonder how they do it?'

'Unreal transfer,' replied the Doctor. 'Has to be.'

'One problem.'

'What?'

'This part of the galaxy doesn't discover the principles of unreal transfer for another century and a half. I looked it up: it's a matter of historic record.'

'Then the history books have got it wrong,' said the Doctor. 'Not for the first time,' he added.

The game of squash was replaced in the bubble by other scenes, which were all fantastically manipulated in their turn. Then Pangol appeared, floating inside the bubble. Or so it seemed. He smiled and waved at his audience.

'Sorry, ladies and gentlemen,' he said genially, 'but that completes the demonstration for the moment. See you soon.'

An expression of alarm crossed his face.

'I hope,' he added – as one of his arms detached itself from his body and flew off into space.

The audience reacted in shocked horror, which rapidly degenerated into laughter when Pangol, apparently undisturbed by the loss of a limb, tried to grab it as it floated past him. The laughter continued when one of his legs fell off and started to do a dance on its own. Eventually all that was left of Pangol was his head, which began to grow larger and larger until it filled the whole bubble. At the end there was just his eye. The bubble had become one enormous staring eyeball.

'See you soon,' said Pangol – and winked.

The audience applauded enthusiastically.

'You still say it's unreal transfer?' queried Romana.

The Doctor shook his head. 'I don't know,' he admitted. 'But if it isn't, then someone's found out how to do some very strange things with a tachyon generator.'

'He's got a lot of talent, that boy of yours,' remarked Brock.

He and Morix were still sitting in the boardroom. They had been watching Pangol's display of tachyonics on one of the video screens. Morix, who seemed to have recovered slightly, indicated that Brock should turn off the monitor.

'Take my advice, old friend,' said the Terran, leaning across to depress the button on the desk console. 'Sell this place. Get rid of it. Buy a new future for your race.'

'It's very tempting,' agreed Morix.

'It's the sensible thing to do.'

'From where does this offer originate?'

Brock shrugged. 'It's not important who wants to buy the planet,' he observed. 'Just be grateful that somebody does.'

'Who are they?'

'A group,' he said. 'A syndicate.'

'Which group? What syndicate?'

'Does it matter?'

Obviously it did.

Brock sighed; he could see trouble looming ahead. 'Very well,' he replied at last. 'If you must know, it's a Foamasi syndicate which has made the offer.'

Morix stared at him in amazement. 'Foamasi?' he cried, seemingly rejuvenated by the sudden access of adrenalin in his veins.

'Their galactic credits are as good as anyone else's,' pointed out Brock. 'Better, in fact. Since no one else can breathe your atmosphere – only a reptilian species whose genes were randomly modified by the effect of radioactivity caused by Argolin missiles.'

Morix did not reply for a moment. He was trying to take in the news. 'You mean,' he said at last, 'that it is because of our missiles that the Foamasi can breathe our polluted air?'

'It's about the only air they can breathe.' Brock laughed without humour. 'Ironic, isn't it, when you come to think about it? But that's the way it is. As a result of the war you waged, you made your own planet uninhabitable for your own race. Yet at the same time you transformed your enemies into the only biological heirs to your own world. At least the Foamasi could live out there on the surface of your planet. They won't need all that protective shielding you can't afford to maintain.'

Morix closed his eyes. Oh, my poor Argolis, he thought, is it we who are guilty of destroying you?

'What do they want with this planet?' he asked.

'Who knows?' replied Brock. 'And who cares what a bunch of asthmatic green snakes with legs want with a place like this? I say they're welcome to it.'

'My people will care. Pangol will care. It's hard for an Argolin to live with defeat. And to be forced to sell our world to our enemies – isn't that the ultimate dishonour?'

'Then you will sell?' demanded Brock.

Morix did not reply.

'Look, I'm just an accountant,' continued the other. 'Not a warrior. I don't understand grand emotions. For me a defeat is when the books don't balance. Dishonour is when you lose to the galactic tax collectors.'

Suddenly tired, Morix leaned his head on his hands. A crystal, one of the jewels with which all the Argolin dressed their hair, fell on to the table. Brock forbore to pick it up.

The Doctor and Romana joined the crowd of excited holidaymakers who surrounded Pangol when he emerged from the tachyon generator.

'It is a well known fact that the tachyon was first discovered on Earth,' insisted an intense lady. She was dressed in a seamless, fluorescent suit that fitted her like a second skin and she wore a hat that looked as if it were made out of living moss (which it was). She glared accusingly at Pangol.

'Agreed,' said Pangol. 'The tachyon particle was

37

ïirst hypothesised on Terra. But that's as far as they got. They never developed it. They never did anything about it.'

'What I'm saying,' insisted the lady in the moss hat, 'is that it is quite wrong of you to claim tachyonics as an Argolin science. We on Earth could have done all this—' she waved a set of jewelled nails at the generator '—if we had wanted.'

Pangol once again blandly agreed with the woman. But Romana, who was watching him, could see the rage boiling inside the young Argolin. It was like a forest fire: one day it would get out of control. How you hate all these visitors to your planet, she thought!

'Excuse me,' said the Doctor. 'May I ask a question?'

The lady in the fluorescent suit attempted to wither the tall, oddly dressed figure with a glance. In the course of her seven marriages it was a technique she had employed successfully to reduce her husbands to nerveless wrecks. But the Doctor, unwithered, unwrecked, smiled aimiably.

'Argolin science! It doesn't exist,' she declared. And she turned on her heel and left.

Pangol fought to regain his self control. He shrugged. 'Must be one of those Terran nationalists,' he said at last.

But the Doctor wasn't interested in politics. 'As I understand it,' he observed, 'a tachyon travels faster than the speed of light.'

'Correct.'

'So it follows that a tachyon field can be made to arrive at Point B *before* it has left Point A. Am I right?'

'Quite right,' agreed Pangol.

'Or put it another way,' went on the Doctor. 'A tachyon field can move backwards or forwards in

38

Time without relation to the space it occupies .'

'Indeed.'

'Which is all very interesting,' said the Doctor. 'That is, if you're interested in hypothetical particles. But it doesn't explain what went on when the generator projected your image – or was it really you? – into that thing up there.' He pointed to the bubble screen.

Pangol's eyes were wary. 'What did you say your name was?' he asked.

'I didn't,' said the Doctor. 'Anyway we were talking about your generator.'

'If you like I could show you the wave equations that define the creation of three-dimensional tachyonic images—' began Pangol.

'I like,' replied the Doctor. He took a stub of a pencil and a crumpled piece of paper from his pocket. 'Here. Use this.'

5

Intruders

A bitter wind blew, colder than charity. Even if you were protected by a heated space suit, it still seemed to chill you to the bone. Or perhaps that was just the effect of the dead landscape – an immense plain broken here and there by short, jagged outcrops of rock: mostly quartz and granite. Everything else had been worn away.

The surface of Argolis was gritty underfoot and covered with a kind of coarse dust, a couple of centimetres thick. It was like walking on ash, which is precisely what the surface layer was composed of – ash and cold cinders.

The colours which blazed in the sky overhead somehow made the scene look even more desolate. Once outside the Leisure Hive you realized that the air – or at least the gales that roared across the planet – were full of tiny fragments of glittering dust which reflected and refracted light from Argolis' suns.

Somewhere in this brilliant world of colour ash stirred and rose and was snatched away in the wind. Webbed feet left tracks which were instantly erased. Something was moving cautiously across the barren plain in the direction of the Hive.

They – for by now it was clear there were at least two of them – had planned their advance with care. Out of sight of the great observation domes, which erupted from the building like enormous transparent blisters and were crowded with holidaymakers, they approached the rear of the Hive. They followed the wall round to where the storerooms, offices, laboratories and other service areas were located. There they attached a sensor to the exterior wall, and listened.

There was the sound of movement within; some Argolin was checking equipment in a storeroom. They waited patiently under the lee of the wall, their breathing harsh and laboured in the poisonous air of Argolis. At last, when their detector confirmed that the Argolin had gone and the storeroom beyond was empty, they began work.

Getting into the Hive took a matter of minutes. They attached a small box to the wall, then drew it slowly down the side of the Hive, so that it traced out a circle – a circle large enough to permit their access. Inside, in the darkness of the storeroom, the circular lines glowed and the wall itself bubbled as if attacked by acid. When the circle was complete, a slight pressure from a clawed hand was enough to push the segment of wall inwards. The figures entered the Hive. They replaced the cut fragment of wall and, using the same device, reversed the cutting process. The opening was sealed shut, and to the casual observer there was no sign it had ever existed.

It was the duty of the maintenance guides to monitor all functions of the Leisure Hive 20·5 hours a day. (Incidentally 20·5 hours *was* the length of an Argolin day.) Any change in atmospheric pressures or increase in radiation levels – in fact any variation in the physical status of the Hive – and lights would begin to flash in the maintenance control room. Alarms sounded. Emergency routines went into immediate operation. The extent of the damage (if any) was assessed, and repairs put in hand.

A maintenance guide reported to his superior: 'There appears to be a small break in the fabric of the exterior wall.'

'Whereabouts?'

'Storeroom area.'

The senior maintenance guide checked all his instruments. They confirmed his assistant's report. He was just about to seal off that section of the Hive and order in a maintenance crew, when the alarm stopped. The guide rechecked his instruments. They now registered no activity above acceptable safety parameters. Apparently the Hive was operating normally again.

'Must be a temporary equipment failure,' he concluded. 'Order everyone to stand down.'

Such failures were becoming routine now that Argolis Leisure Planet Inc. was being forced to economize on regular maintenance work.

In the boardroom Morix lay in his chair, gasping for breath. His face was ashen, his eyes closed, his breathing stertorous.

Brock was alarmed. 'We can't just stand here and let him die,' he told Klout. 'We have to do something.'

Klout indicated the desk console.

Brock played a tattoo on a button on the console. According to the Argolin script, it should have instantly summoned Medical Services. Apparently it didn't. Nothing happened.

'Where is everyone?' complained Brock. 'Their Chairman, their Heresiarch, is dying. You'd think someone would care. But no one seems to give a damn, except us.'

He lifted Morix's limp hand and let it flop back on the arm of his chair like a dead fish.

'Go and see if you can find anybody,' he told Klout.

Klout didn't move.

Brock smiled. 'Silly of me. I forgot,' he said. 'I'll go. But before he could get to the door it slid open and Vargos and Dorant, two of the Argolin, entered.

'About time,' snapped Brock. 'Morix is much worse.'

Vargos and Dorant ignored the Terran. They crossed to the Heresiarch, and while one took his pulse, the other lifted his eyelids.

'How long has he been like this?' demanded Vargos.

'It all happened a moment ago,' replied Brock. 'He suddenly…collapsed.'

Dorant felt for the vein on Morix's neck. 'It's nearly time,' he told Vargos.

'Is there anything we can do?' asked Brock.

'Nothing.'

Vargos went to a wall cupboard and took out a package, which turned out to contain something that resembled a silver plastic sleeping bag.

'Aren't you going to do anything for him,' demanded the Terran. 'The man's obviously very sick.'

The two Argolin ignored the Terrans. They took their places one on either side of the Argolin leader. Together they levered him into a sitting position. For a moment Morix sat bolt upright, his eyes closed, his breathing sounding as if his lungs were a pair of punctured bellows. Then suddenly the bellows stopped. The Heresiarch of Argolis ceased breathing. His head fell forward onto the table and the last remaining crystals which glittered in his hair fell out. His hair turned in a second from gold to white. Morix was dead.

'Good grief,' said Brock, 'is that how all you Argolin die?'

Swiftly the two Argolin slid the corpse into the silver bag and zipped it up. While they were thus occupied, Brock looked at Klout and motioned for him to go. Klout slipped out of the boardroom.

In the Great Hall the Doctor and Romana listened intently to Pangol's explanation of the working of his tachyon generator. The Doctor was puzzled. It seemed to him there was a devil of a lot the fellow wasn't explaining.

'I'm not surprised,' said Romana. 'Look at his audience. Do they look as if they'd understand Cerenkov radiation wave equations?'

'All the same,' insisted the Doctor, 'he's obviously made some kind of breakthrough in tachyonics. So why not tell us about it? Why not flaunt it?'

'Modesty,' suggested Romana.

'Rubbish,' declared the Doctor.

'Commercial reason?'

'Possibly.' The Doctor gazed thoughtfully at the generator. 'You know I wish I could get inside there and take a look at the negative-image chamber.'

Unknown to the Doctor and Romana that was precisely what someone was doing.

The shuttle from the hyperspace liner from Terra descended onto the surface of Argolis. The first person to leave the craft, once the door was open, was Mena. She was still clutching the black globe which was chained to her wrist.

Mena had been informed of Morix's death during the hyperspace trip, and in true Argolin fashion had taken the news without a flicker of emotion. She had bowed her head in silence for a moment, for she had respected her consort. Then with quiet courtesy she had thanked the Captain of the hyperspace liner who had left his bridge to break the news to her. He had attempted to express his sympathy, but the words had died on his lips under the gaze of those impassive Argolin eyes.

'I'll never understand the Argolin,' he complained to his second officer when he returned to the bridge. 'They're cold.'

'It's all because of their warrior ethic,' explained the second officer, who would often while away the long watches by reading galactic history and anthropology. ' "Sorrow, pain and fear are weaknesses in a warrior",' he quoted. ' "Eliminate them." That's the First Precept of Theron the Terrible.'

'Good thing there aren't many Argolin left, if you ask me,' he went on. 'Otherwise they might feel inclined to put into practice Theron's Second Precept.'

'What's that?'

' "War is the right and duty of every Argolin",' quoted the second officer.

Mena hastened up the hover pavement to the First Observation Hall. Ignoring, as all the Argolin did, the ever-shifting parade of colours above her head, she made her way to the boardroom of the Leisure Hive.

There she was met by Brock, full of sympathy and ready to proffer a shoulder to weep on. But as he soon discovered, the Argolin do not weep.

'Morix did his duty as an Argolin should,' she declared, cutting short his condolences.

'The Heresiarch died well,' said Vargos, intoning the ritual phrases for the death of a leader of the Argolin. 'And may the next Heresiarch die as bravely.'

'Praise be to Theron,' murmured Dorant.

Mena bowed her head.

The moment of sentiment over, she took her seat in the chair in which Morix had died. 'In view of the death of my consort,' she said, 'and in accordance with the laws of my people, I automatically become Chairwoman of the Leisure Hive and Heresiarch of Argolis. Agreed?'

'Agreed,' said Vargos and Dorant.

'Wait a minute,' objected Brock. 'Surely we ought to discuss this—'

'There is nothing to discuss,' observed the new Chairwoman. 'The succession is decided. And now to business....'

To Brock's amazement they then discussed the day-to-day routine of the running of the Leisure Hive during her absence on Terra, as if nothing had happened.

At last Vargos asked: 'Where is the Earth scientist? I thought you were bringing him with you?'

Mena explained that Hardin and his assistant were arriving by the next shuttle. She unlocked the chain from her wrist and slid the black globe on the table.

'Here it is,' she said. 'I thought I ought to bring it with me. A holocrystal of the first trials.'

'What trials?' asked Brock. 'What's been going on behind your accountant's back?'

'Hardin has found a better use for Argolin tachyonics than those games with which Pangol amuses the holidaymakers,' announced Mena.

'What better use? What's this Hardin fellow discovered?' demanded the accountant.

'He has shown us how to manipulate Time.'

Using the stub of a pencil, the Doctor was trying to work out the various mathematical equations which

Pangol punched out on the console of the generator. The equations appeared on the bubble screen.

'Satisfied?' asked Pangol who was growing weary of the Doctor's persistent questions.

'Frankly,' replied the Doctor, 'no.'

'What's wrong? Can't you do the sums?'

Pangol winked at the crowd of holidaymakers, who roared with laughter. Here was an unexpected bonus to their day – the discomfiture of a would-be expert.

'All you're giving me,' said the Doctor patiently, 'is the building blocks of tachyonics. General theory's all very well, but let's have a few specifics.'

'Like what?'

'Temporal ratios. Duration constants. Re-duplication fields.'

Pangol's eyes narrowed. This strange-looking visitor was beginning to ask some awkward questions. He seemed to know altogether too much about tachyonics for his own good. Somehow he had to be headed off.

'One of these days, when we've got more time,' lied Pangol, 'I'll be happy to show you around the machine.'

'Any time you like,' agreed the Doctor. 'The sooner the better.'

But a balding Terran clad in a glimmering smock had other ideas. It had been his wife's idea to come to Argolis. The place was all very colourful no doubt, but personally he was bored stiff. The generator was the first thing he had seen which promised to provide a good laugh.

'Forget theories,' said the Terran. 'What I want to know is – does that thing really work, or is it all a fake?'

Gratefully Pangol turned his attention to the new

questioner. 'Visitor Loman,' he said, reading the name badge attached to the man's smock, 'you think we might have been using edited recordings in our demonstration, do you?'

'You're dead right!'

'Rubbish,' snapped the Doctor. 'The whole thing's real – that's what worries me.'

Pangol ignored his intervention. 'Perhaps you'd care to try the machine for yourself, Mr Loman,' he suggested. 'Take my place inside.'

Mr Loman stared at the generator, his enthusiasm for the prospect waning fast.

'Having second thoughts?' queried Pangol maliciously.

'No, of course not,' replied the man with noticeable lack of conviction.

The watching holidaymakers roared with laughter.

Pangol slid open the doors to the central chamber of the generator and invited Loman to enter. 'There's nothing to it,' he told the Terran. 'The machine does it all. Just stand in the image chamber and try to relax.'

Loman smiled weakly, but he managed a cheery wave to the crowd outside before Pangol closed the doors.

Pangol busied himself at the control console. 'First,' he told his audience, 'the projection.'

Suddenly a startled Loman could be seen floating upside down in the bubble screen.

The crowd applauded.

'Two temporally coincident Mr Lomans are now in existence,' explained Pangol; 'one inside the image chamber, the other – as you can see – within the bubble.

'Now,' he went on, 'we can manipulate the one without injuring the other.'

He began to punch in instructions to the computer. The audience stared at the image of Loman, now right side up, floating in the bubble. Apparently full of confidence, the Terran began to wave at his fellow holidaymakers. He pulled faces and clowned around to the amusement of the audience.

Suddenly a look of agony crossed his face.

His left arm detached itself from his shoulder and floated off into space. But unlike Pangol's earlier demonstration, the amputation was followed by a great fountain of blood from his shoulder. The right leg detached itself from Loman's body. Again it was accompanied by a cataract of blood. The bubble screen was by now spattered with scarlet.

The crowd screamed.

Detecting the change of tone, Pangol glanced up from the computer console and stared in horror at the one-armed, one-legged, lifeless figure of Loman floating above the generator.

'Get him out of there!' shouted the Doctor. 'Hurry, for Heaven's sake! Open up this thing!'

Pangol fumbled with the catch, then slid aside the doors of the generator. The Doctor entered.

'Who is that man?' Pangol asked Romana.

'The Doctor.'

'Is he a scientist?'

Romana nodded. Experience had taught her to keep explanation down to a minimum. In any case, how did you explain the Doctor? Even his fellow Time Lords preferred to keep him at arm's length.

'He must be the scientist Mena decided to import from Terra,' said Pangol. 'That would by why he was asking all those questions about tachyonics.'

Fortunately Romana was required neither to confirm nor deny the charge, for just then the

49

Doctor emerged from the generator. He was looking rather shaken.

'How is he?' demanded Pangol.

'Dead.'

'Dead? But that's impossible.'

'Not if you've just had an arm and a leg torn off,' snapped the Doctor, who was in no mood to suffer fools gladly.

Pangol stared at him aghast. 'You mean, what we saw on the bubble screen really happened? It's impossible.'

'That's the second time you've said it,' observed the Doctor. 'Go and see for yourself.'

'But you don't understand, the only way it could happen would be if the generator had been repolarized. And that would mean the reversal of the whole image function.'

'Tell that to the poor devil in there,' said the Doctor tartly. 'I'm sure he'll be impressed.'

With Romana at his heels the Doctor began to elbow his way through the excited mob. Meanwhile, using his communicator, Pangol ordered immediate medical facilities, then he spoke to Security at some length.

The Doctor and Romana had found a quiet corner. They were hidden from the mob's view by one of the crystal statues of Argolin heroes which dotted the Great Recreation Hall. They were waiting for the hubbub to die down.

'I don't know about you,' remarked the Doctor, 'but I've had enough of Argolis. Let's try and work our way back to the TARDIS and get out of here.' He peered through the crystal pelvis of the statue. 'I don't think anyone has noticed us yet.'

'Wrong,' said Romana.

'Eh?'

Romana nudged him. The Doctor turned round to face three large Argolin Security guides, who were looking down on him with a distinct lack of cheer.

'Madam Chairman,' said the smallest guide, 'wishes to see you, sir.'

'Now, sir,' said the other two.

At that moment Mena was in the boardroom showing Vargos, Dorant and Brock a holographic recording of the experiments which Hardin had done on Terra. They were watching Hardin and his assistant, Stimson, helping an elderly lady into a chair in their laboratory, which was placed in the midst of a set of tachyon projectors, all wired to small individual generators.

The phantom Hardin in the holograph turned and spoke directly to his audience. 'In this experiment,' he explained, 'I propose to demonstrate the temporal anomaly inherent in the tachyon.'

Brock, however, was not impressed. 'Is that what Morix sent you all the way to Terra for?' he demanded. 'What a waste of money!'

Unperturbed, the holographic Hardin continued his lecture, while his assistant checked the apparatus: 'As you all know, the tachyon travels faster than the speed of light, thus creating in its path, in whichever direction it may travel, a temporal anomaly. In other words, the structure of Time itself changes as a tachyon passes.

'The theory behind my work, therefore, is simple. By controlling the emission and direction of tachyon particles within a confined space – for example, within the area bounded by these tachyon projectors—' he indicated the projectors '—we should be able to affect the flow of Time itself within that area.'

The holographic Hardin nodded to his assistant who switched on the generators. Soon the projector tubes began to glow with a strange flickering light.

'I can't see anything happening,' grumbled Brock. 'If you ask me, the whole thing's a waste of time. When's it supposed to start?'

'Watch,' said Mena.

Unimpressed, Brock watched. Then suddenly he leaned forward unable to believe his eyes.

The old lady was changing. Her face began to fill out; her white hair gradually darkened; wrinkles vanished; the colour of youth returned to her skin. The woman was growing younger before their eyes. In a matter of minutes she had shed twenty years.

After a while they saw that an attractive young Terran woman now sat where once the old lady had been. They wore the same clothes. They were unmistakably the same person. Yet one was fifty years younger than the other.

'Rejuvenation,' said Mena. 'Complete cellular rejuvenation. That's what Hardin has achieved. He's perfected a technique capable of reversing the flow of Time within a relatively small space – a space large enough to encompass one human being. The result is that person grows younger. Put it another way – Hardin seems to have discovered the Fountain of Youth.'

'I don't believe it,' declared Brock.

'You saw.'

'I don't believe what I saw.' Brock was obviously shaken by what he had just witnessed. 'I mean, if it's true—'

'Can you doubt it?'

'—then it's incredible,' he added weakly.

Mena smiled. 'Think of it,' she said. 'It could revolutionize the future of Argolis. Can't you see the publicity? ''Come to Argolis – and regain your lost youth. Grow young again on Argolis.'' '

'There has to be a snag,' objected Brock.

'Why?'

'Because there always is.'

As if to make a liar out of him, the holographic recording kept repeating the two images – the old woman and the young one: before and after. Those in the boardroom watched again and again as fifty years fell from her shoulders.

It was just at that moment that the three Argolin Security guides ushered the Doctor and Romana into the boardroom.

'Who are they?' asked Mena.

'The scientist Hardin and his assistant, Madam Chairman,' said the senior guide. 'You told us to look out for them, and Pangol was sure—'

'That isn't Hardin,' cried Mena. 'That man's an impostor!'

'Not exactly,' objected the Doctor, anxious to keep the record straight. 'That is to say, it is true that I am not this Hardin chap. Whoever he may be. On the other hand, I never claimed to be him. Did I?'

The Argolin regarded him stonily. They did not reply.

'No,' said the Doctor. 'I didn't.'

'We can conclude therefore that a very natural mistake has been made which,' he added genially, 'I am prepared to overlook.'

'He was taking notes at Pangol's lecture on the generator,' insisted the senior Argolin Security guide. 'Everyone was sure he was Mr Hardin.'

'And now he's seen these experiments,' said Brock.

'Experiments?' queried Romana, trying to brazen it out. 'What experiments? We haven't seen any experiments. Have we, Doctor?'

But the hologram continued to cut from the old

lady to the young one, from before to after.

No one spoke.

One of the video screens on the wall of the boardroom flashed into life. Pangol could be seen in the mortuary. Behind him was an Argolin pathologist who was inspecting the mortal remains of Mr Loman.

'There's been sabotage at the generator,' announced Pangol. 'One of the visitors has been killed. Murdered. Someone reversed the image function in the generator.'

'That's all we need,' groaned Brock. 'A murder in the Leisure Hive. You just wait and see the effect it has on the bookings.'

Mena took charge. She ordered Pangol to have the body prepared for immediate repatriation to Mr Loman's home planet. Which in this case was Earth.

'And tell our mortician,' she went on, 'that I want his best cosmetic job. The dead visitor must return looking as if he died peacefully in his sleep.'

While Mena was thus engaged, the Doctor and Romana began to edge towards the door. By the time she was ready to continue her questioning of them, they had slipped away. 'Go after them!' she commanded. 'I want them brought back here.'

In the corridor the Doctor and Romana met a Security guide.

'Can I help you?' he asked.

'No, thank you,' replied the Doctor. 'We're just leaving. But you had better be on the look-out for two unidentified aliens. Stand by for a description from your leader.'

Like a good Argolin, the Security guide came to attention, alert for any instructions which might come over his communicator. Right on cue Mena's voice could be heard saying: 'Attention. Attention. Attention. All Security guides to be on the look-out

54

for two visitors. Description – one tall curly-haired humanoid (male) in the company of one smaller blonde humanoid (female).'

The Doctor and Romana took to their heels before the Argolin could match the description to them.

'That experiment was faked,' gasped Romana when they paused for breath by one of the pillars in the Great Recreation Hall.

'I know,' wheezed the Doctor, leaning against the crystal statue of Lismar the Champion. The ancient Argolin hero had been caught by the sculptor in an agressive pose, his sword at the ready. 'Two discontinuous holographs had been edited together. I noticed very faint interference patterns.'

'I noticed the necklace.'

'What necklace?'

'The one she wore. Look,' explained Romana, 'both the old woman and the young one wore the same clothes. But they forgot to match their jewellery. Different necklaces.'

The Doctor thought about it. 'Odd when you think about it,' he said at last. 'On the one hand you have something going very wrong inside their tachyon generator. At the same time someone on Earth has been faking experiments in tachyonics. Are the two events connected? If so, how and why?'

Romana could see the danger signals. The Doctor was beginning to become interested in Argolis and its problems. 'Let's get back to the TARDIS before we land in real trouble,' she declared, painfully aware that she had said that frequently in the past – all to no avail.

Nothing daunted, she seized the ends of the Doctor's scarf and proceeded to drag him in the direction of the police box. Unfortunately it was not until she got to the door of the TARDIS that she realized she was towing in her wake, not the Doctor as she had thought, but the crystal statue of Lismar the Champion. The Doctor's scarf was wound round the Champion's neck. Meanwhile the Doctor himself was over the other side of the Great Recreation Hall, examining the generator.

'Doctor!' cried Romana. 'Doctor! Come on!'

But she was too late. The Doctor was already opening the door of the generator.

'Won't be a jiff!' he called. 'Back in a second!'

And with a cheery wave he popped inside the generator and closed the door behind him.

Romana ran over and tried to force open the door. But it wouldn't budge; the Doctor must have tripped the catch from the inside. Romana pounded desperately on the door.

'Come out!' she yelled. 'Come out of there! We're in enough trouble as it is.'

But the door was soundproof.

Inside the generator the Doctor could hear nothing, except for the gentle humming of the generator itself. The Doctor was standing inside a black dodeca-hedron.

The interior of the image chamber was lit by a subdued light which seemed to emanate from the black glass panels lining the walls. Curious, the Doctor inspected the panels. They fitted neatly into each other, revealing no sign of join or crack. With the aid of his sonic screwdriver, he managed to prise off one of the panels. It came away easily once the magnetic seal had been broken. Behind it lay no labyrinth of wires and tubes and micro-circuits. Instead there was a kind of infinitude. An emptiness. A nothingness, cold as Space itself, in which drifted slow wraiths of what looked like smoke which crackled periodically with tachyon emissions.

'Fascinating,' said the Doctor.

While Romana was busy trying to force the door of the generator, the diagnostic panel by the control console suddenly flickered into life. On it appeared the words: SENTIENT LIFE FORM INSIDE THE GENERATOR. FAIL SAFE MECHANISM IN OPERATION.

Finding the door immovable, Romana called to a group of passing holidaymakers for help. They came running over at once and shoved and pushed at her command. But even their united strength could not move the door. It was locked fast.

Meanwhile something with green, scaly, clawlike hands took advantage of the uproar to issue fresh instructions to the computer. The instructions, which appeared on the diagnostic panel of the console, consisted of only five words — but they spelt death to any occupant of the image chamber: OVER-RIDE FAIL SAFE MECHANISM.

The faint humming of the generator changed key. A different note could now be heard. The machine was running. Its operations were random and lethal.

Someone in the crowd screamed and pointed at the bubble screen.

Romana looked up. In the bubble she saw the Doctor, his face contorted with agony. He was gradually being torn apart.

6

Hardin

As Pangol and Brock entered the Great Recreation Hall, the latter pointed: 'There he is!'

Pangol stared in horror at the figure of the Doctor trapped in the bubble screen. Both arms had been torn from their sockets and a leg was floating beside him.

'Help me get him out!' screamed Romana.

Pangol ran across to the control console and pressed the door release button, while Brock lent his considerable weight to forcing the door. But nothing happened. The door remained jammed.

'Switch off the power,' suggested Romana.

'I can't,' replied Pangol.

'Why not?'

'I don't know. The computer must be malfunctioning.'

'But there must be something we can do.'

'You could try shorting the servo-lock mechanism,' said a familiar voice. 'I did. It worked in my case.'

Romana and Pangol turned round to find the Doctor standing behind them.

'How did you get out?' they demanded.

But the Doctor was admiring himself in the bubble screen above the generator. There he could be seen to be in no fewer than six separate pieces. 'Handsome chap,' he remarked smugly.

'If you're out here,' demanded Romana, 'who's that up there?'

'One of those famous tachyon images. It'll fade soon. Look.'

They saw the figure of the dismembered Doctor gradually begin to fade.

'How did you get out?' asked Pangol.

'Through a hole in the back.'

'But there isn't one.'

'There is now,' replied the Doctor.

When Hardin arrived on Argolis with his assistant, Stimson, he was surprised to find they were not expected. Not that he had hoped to be met by a welcoming committee, but some acknowledgement of his existence would have done wonders for his confidence. Instead they stepped off the shuttle to find that no one even knew their names. Obviously Mena had failed to warn any of the staff. Why?

Hardin, who was a compulsive worrier, began to worry. He left Stimson to enjoy the colours of Argolis in the First Observation Hall, while he made his way to the boardroom.

There he found Mena alone, sitting in the Heresiarch's chair, and watching the antics in progress around the tachyon generator. The bank of video screens facing her showed the scene from several different angles.

'My dear,' he said, pleased to see her again.

Mena corrected him gently. 'Madam Chairman.'

'Madam Chairman?'

'Morix, my consort, is dead. I am now the ruler of Argolis.'

Hardin nodded. He had heard the news from the telecast aboard the hyperspace liner. 'Does it make any difference to our – relationship?' he asked.

'I am no longer a free agent,' explained Mena. 'I am now responsible for this planet. The past is past.'

'For the time being at any rate,' she added.

'I understand,' said Hardin. 'I shall not embarrass you.'

Abruptly Mena changed the subject. Anything to distance herself from those few mad days she had spent on Terra with this man. She pointed to the video screen, where two Security guides could be seen dragging the indignant Doctor away from a strange blue box. 'Do you know this man?' she asked.

Hardin shook his head.

'He seems to be some kind of scientist. A Doctor no less. He claims to know something about tachyonics.' She looked directly at Hardin. 'He mentioned temporal instability,' she went on. 'How much does he know?'

That, thought Hardin, was precisely the question.

'Anyway it would do no harm to keep him out of circulation for a while,' Mena said. 'At least until we're ready.'

'Ready for what?'

'For a full scale experiment.' She smiled at him. 'You told me yourself on Terra that all the work had been done: you had solved all the problems.'

'Yes,' replied Hardin uneasily. 'Most of the problems.'

Much to his relief their conversation was interrupted by the Security guides, who entered with the Doctor and Romana. Brock brought up the rear.

Mena lost no time in getting down to business. 'You are the Doctor?' she enquired.

The Doctor acknowledged the fact.

'Where do you come from?'

'Gallifrey.'

'I've never heard of the place.'

'I'm not surprised,' agreed the Doctor. 'It's a small, remote planet. Why should you have heard of it?'

60

'And we're overdue there,' explained Romana. 'We ought to be on our way now, oughtn't we, Doctor?'

The Doctor took the hint. 'Yes, indeed,' he said. 'Time we were off.'

But the Security guides blocked their path.

'Goodbye,' said the Doctor hopefully.

Mena ignored their attempts to leave. 'Tell me about Gallifrey?' she asked. 'Do they experiment with Time there?'

'Time?' queried the Doctor, as if he had never heard of such a thing.

Mena did not reply.

'We,' he said, 'that is to say, certain – ah – academics on Gallifrey have been known to engage in certain – ah – academic experiments regarding temporal matters. Time and space. Things like that. Nothing important.'

'Just experiments,' interjected Romana. 'Of no interest to anybody.'

'None,' agreed the Doctor. 'Why, Gallifrey abandoned tachyonics ages ago.'

'When we developed warp matrix engineering,' added Romana – and then wished she had bitten off her tongue. If the Argolin knew anything about temporal mechanics, then they must realize the significance of her remark.

But fortunately Mena had other things on her mind. She turned to Hardin. 'Mr Hardin, since these two persons have come from a planet where such matters are obviously not unknown,' she suggested, 'perhaps they could be of assistance to you.'

Aware that he had no alternative but to comply with her plan, Hardin nodded. He did not, however, look happy at the prospect. Neither did the Doctor.

'It will demonstrate your good faith, Doctor,' said

Mena.

I wasn't aware I was required to demonstrate anything,' he replied. 'Still, if you insist—'

'I do.'

The Doctor bowed.

'You saw the recording of Mr Hardin's time experiments?' she enquired.

'Hardly.'

'A glimpse only,' agreed Romana.

'Then perhaps you ought to take another look,' proposed Mena. 'Mr Hardin will take you to the laboratory and show you his work in detail.'

'Love to,' said the Doctor. 'Unfortunately we must be going.'

'We have a schedule to keep,' explained Romana.

'You have time,' declared Mena. 'If need be, all the time in the world.' The threat in her voice was unmistakable.

Hardin's heart sank. The last thing he wanted was an expert – or even a knowledgeable amateur – checking on the results of his experiments.

But the Doctor wasn't prepared to give up without a fight. 'One thing I don't understand,' he observed, 'is why Mr Hardin's work should be so important to the Argolin.'

'I would have thought that was obvious,' replied Mena. 'As the first Leisure Planet to offer a course of painless physical regeneration to its customers, we'll make a fortune. We'll be the most popular place in the Galaxy. We'll be turning down bookings.'

'Why is it I don't believe you?' said the Doctor.

In the maze of narrow maintenance tunnels underneath the Leisure Hive some thing moved. A creature with green scales and clawed hands eased its way along a passage until it found what it was looking for – a wall panel. The creature swiftly unscrewed the panel. Inside was a web of wires and fibres: the fibre-optic system. Other panels gave access to the various communication and life-support systems of the Hive. They were the arteries of Argolis. The creature deposited a small hexagonal box amongst the wires, and then replaced the panel.

Mena threw back her head and roared with laughter. 'You're very shrewd, Doctor,' she said. 'And very forth-right. So be it. Perhaps you deserve to learn our secret.'

She pressed a button on the desk console. Part of the wall slid back to reveal the Argolin landscape as it had been before the Foamasi War. The sheer beauty of the scene made Romana and the Doctor gasp in wonder.

'It will take three centuries before the Argolin can safely walk out onto the surface of our planet,' she continued. 'Three centuries before we can claim our inheritance.'

'And what are you going to do meanwhile?' demanded the Doctor. 'Stay in the Leisure Hive for three hundred years? Bring up generations of Argolin here? Incidentally,' he added, 'where are they? I haven't seen any children here.'

Mena smiled sadly. 'There are none,' she said. 'Every war extracts its price, and the Foamasi War exacted the most terrible price of all. We Argolin are sterile. We cannot produce children. There are no future generations. The only hope for us is to find some way of regenerating ourselves.'

She reactivated the holographic crystal which contained the recording of Hardin's experiment with the old woman. As they watched, the woman changed from age to youth. Mena stared at the scene as if hypnotized by it.

'Hardin's work offers my race its only hope of

survival,' she said at last. 'Perhaps in time we will be able to rebuild Argolis and fill the Hive with our children.'

Inside a wall panel in the maze of narrow maintenance tunnels underneath the Leisure Hive there was an explosion. One of the arteries of Argolis had been severed.

Suddenly the holographic crystal went black. The picture vanished.

Frowning, Mena ran a diagnostic check through the computer. 'Inter-fibral malfunction,' she diagnosed at last. 'The line has gone down.'

'Another accident?' queried the Doctor. 'Like the one this morning that killed that poor chap in the generator?'

Mena did not reply.

'I think someone is trying to sabotage the Hive,' said the Doctor.

A strange expression crossed Mena's face. Her eyes glazed. She staggered and would have fallen had not Hardin caught her. She clutched the table. A crystal dropped from her hair.

'Mena,' he cried.

The Doctor took charge. 'Sit her back in the chair,' he ordered. He took her pulse and began to examine her, paying particular attention to the skin round her eyes and the flesh on the backs of her hands.

'What's the matter with her?' asked Hardin anxiously. 'She looks so ill.'

'Old,' said Brock.

'Old?'

'She's just aged about twenty years in a few seconds. Like Morix. I saw what happened to him.'

The Doctor confirmed Brock's diagnosis. 'Most

remarkable,' he agreed. 'There's been a sudden cellular degeneration.'

'I don't understand,' said Hardin.

Mena took his hand in hers and grinned crookedly at him. 'Instant old age,' she said. 'It happens to us all. Sooner or later.' She seemed to revive a little. Her voice grew stronger. 'Now you know why your experiments are so important. To me, most of all. They could save my life.'

Stimson was setting up the experiment at one end of the laboratory. He kept looking over his shoulder at Hardin explaining the intricacies of the equipment to Brock and his silent lawyer who, after being missing for a while, had suddenly reappeared. The presence of the two Terrans worried Stimson. He could see that Hardin was on the verge of a breakdown.

Brock was full of enthusiasm for the project. He clapped Hardin on the shoulder. 'Sounds absolutely fascinating,' he declared. 'A real breakthrough. There is a great commercial future for a reliable rejuvenation technique. Even an unreliable one, come to that. People will clutch at any straw.'

'It's too soon to know how efficient my technique is,' objected Hardin. 'My research is only in its early stages: there's a long way to go yet.'

You don't know how far, he thought.

Brock dismissed the scientist's objections with a wave of his hand. 'Doesn't matter,' he observed. 'No one in their right mind hopes to stay young for ever. Or even wants to. What they'd like is to be able to turn back the clock a bit when they get to middle age. They'll pay through the nose for some machine that will peel off a few years.'

'The Argolin need more than that.'

Brock lowered his voice. 'We all know what the

Argolin need,' he murmured in Hardin's ear. 'But it doesn't mean they'll get it. Could be their metabolism's been speeded up so much that your technique won't work on them.'

'It's not been properly tested yet,' objected Hardin. 'Nobody knows what will happen.'

'Exactly what I'm saying,' declared Brock. 'Isn't that right, Klout?'

Klout did not reply.

Hardin realized that he had never heard him speak.

'If your technique doesn't work on the Argolin, which Heaven forbid,' Brock added piously, 'then we must make sure that your great discovery isn't lost to science for ever. That would be a tragedy.'

Brock's breath was on his cheek. It smelt sweet and faintly chemical.

'All I'm saying,' he continued, 'is that you ought to consider taking on a business partner. Someone who would look after your interests while you concentrated on your work. Someone who would see to it that all mankind reaped the benefit of your genius. Or any kind of kind, come to that. After all there are probably a hundred different intelligent life forms in the galaxy, many of them with access to galactic credits on a large scale. You follow me?'

I'm way ahead of you, thought Hardin.

'Think about it,' said Brock 'that's all I ask.'

He clapped the scientist on the shoulder, then he and his ever-silent lawyer departed.

Hardin turned to Stimson, his face a picture of despair. 'What are we going to do?' he cried.

'Proceed as planned,' replied the other.

It had all seemed so easy when Stimson had approached him on Terra, thought Hardin. He had spent years working on tachyonics. He had even reached a point when he had believed he was on the verge of a great scientific breakthrough. In the laboratory he had several times been able to arrest the flow of time in an experimental organism. Once he had kept a Mayfly alive for three months. Once he had even succeeded in reversing the flow of Time, so that a chicken had been regressed into an egg. But on each and every occasion something had gone wrong. The Mayfly when released had disintegrated into a shower of dust; the egg when opened had disclosed a dead and deformed embryo.

He had been on the verge of giving up his research when Stimson had come to see him at his laboratory. At first he had been flattering about his work and sympathetic that it was haunted by failure.

'All you need,' Stimson had said, 'is finance. A big grant to complete your experiments. Look at this laboratory. Second-hand equipment. No proper facilities. No wonder you haven't succeeded in making a breakthrough.'

The man's words had been balm to Hardin's pride. Nevertheless he had tried to be realistic. 'These days no one will back tachyon experiments,' he had pointed out. 'The tachyon is the Cinderella of sub-atomic particles. A scientific freak. You can prove its existence, but for well over a century no one has found any use for it.'

'Until you,' said Stimson. 'And the Argolin, of course.'

Stimson had arranged it all. He had contacted Morix, Heresiarch of Argolis, Chairman of Argolis Leisure Planet Inc., who had shown a flattering interest in the experiments. Hardin's confidence in his work began to blossom. Morix had even suggested sending his consort to Terra to act as observer.

'We have to keep them interested until you can sort out the bugs in your equipment,' Stimson had said.

'Just give them something to get their teeth into for now. Something to believe in. A successful rejuvenator.'

'I'm not ready for that yet!' Hardin had protested.

But Stimson had been persuasive. 'By the time they get round to putting up any money you'll have solved your technical problems.'

Perhaps it was the result of all those years of struggle and failure, but at the time Stimson's proposition had sounded unorthodox. But not actually criminal. In any case once Hardin had met the beautiful and elegant Mena he had been ready to agree to anything – even Stimson's suggestion that they fake an experiment – in order to keep her beside him for as long as possible.

And the plan had worked. Until now.

Now Mena was dying, and his work – which she still believed might save her – was a fraud and a fake. She would die because he was unable to save her.

Stimson understood Hardin only too well. A brilliant fool, he thought, emotionally unstable – and if he's not handled carefully, he'll destroy everything.

'Hardin,' he said, 'Mena still thinks you are the greatest scientist since Albert Einstein. Don't disappoint her, there's a good fellow. Leave her with some hope.'

But Hardin was adamant. 'No! There have been too many lies. I must tell Mena the truth.'

'Don't be a fool!'

'I will not be party to fraud.'

Stimson lost his temper. 'It's a bit late to think of that now!' he snapped. 'And it's no time to get an attack of the scruples. Remember where we are. On Argolis. Their planet. What do you think the Argolin would do if they discovered we had been leading them up the garden path? Do you really think they'd just slap our wrists and let us go?'

'Mena would never hurt anyone.'

'She's an Argolin, isn't she? They're all a bunch of savages at heart. Always have been. I bet they only took up tachyonics because they thought it would make a better weapon than a radon missile.'

But at that point their argument was interrupted by the arrival of Romana.

'How is Mena?' demanded Hardin.

'The Doctor's with her. He is doing everything he can.'

'I must go to her.'

'No,' said Stimson. 'You'd only be in the way. Best thing we can do is to get this experiment working.' He turned to Romana for support. 'Right, miss?'

'Right. Whatever you do, get the experiment working.'

Stimson shot her a suspicious glance. He detected a satirical note in Romana's voice. What the devil did she know? And who was this self-assured young woman, he wondered? He didn't like the professional way she was inspecting the equipment they had assembled.

'I see you feed the tachyon drive straight into the wafer wave inducer,' she remarked. 'Bit unusual, isn't it? How do you achieve inversion?'

Ouch, thought Stimson, that's all we needed – an expert in tachyonics. Well, time to bale out. Cut your losses. No one would ever accuse him of not knowing when to make a swift exit. He began to edge his way towards the door.

'Well?' asked Romana.

Hardin looked blank for a moment, then with an effort of will he brought his mind back to her question. He mumbled something about the divider circuit automatically dephasing. But in the end the thought of what was happening in the boardroom was too much for him. 'Mena's dying!' he suddenly blurted out. 'There's no way to stop cellular degeneration.'

'First things first,' Romana replied. She was still studying the apparatus. 'Come on now. Tell me how you lock the phase.'

'I don't!' cried Hardin. 'Don't you understand, I can't! The whole contraption doesn't work.'

'Oh, I know that,' said Romana calmly. 'But what I don't understand is why it doesn't. You see, I think it ought to work.'

Stimson stopped an Argolin Holiday guide in the corridor to enquire about shuttles from the planet.

'All fully booked I'm afraid,' said the Argolin, once he had consulted his wrist computer which carried a permanent update on all shuttle flights and bookings.

'But I must get off Argolis now,' insisted the Terran. 'I have urgent business elsewhere. Isn't there any way—?'

The guide was sorry, but only a priority clearance from the Heresiarch herself could wangle him as an extra passenger aboard a shuttle.

'What do I do then?'

The guide pointed out that it was sometimes possible to take over the booking of another off-worlder who had no use for it.

'Like who?' asked Stimson. 'Surely all the holidaymakers are booked on specific flights.'

'Indeed,' agreed the guide. 'But we have other visitors, too. Experts of different kinds. Like the Terran accountant, Mr Brock and his friend. They're booked on the shuttle for every flight next week. They just want to make sure they can leave the planet as soon as their work here is complete. Perhaps if you asked him, he would let you use one of his bookings.'

Stimson thanked the guide and set about finding his fellow Earthling. He decided it was probably safest to wait for Brock in his room.

Eventually Stimson found a cabin which bore on its door the names of Brock and Klout. He knocked. There was no answer. He tried the handle. It was unlocked. He entered.

The cabin was empty. It was quite palatial. But there was no sign of its occupants. No doubt they were still in the boardroom with Mena.

Having found himself a temporary bolthole, Stimson was loath to leave. He was safe here – for the time being, at any rate. Then an idea occurred to him. Perhaps Brock or Klout had left behind some papers, some kind of authorization he could use to get off this damned planet.

Stimson decided to search the place.

Brock's room revealed nothing. There were no papers at all. He entered Klout's room, which was even more spartan. Stimson threw open the wardrobe. What he saw brought a scream to his lips.

Hanging from a hook in the roof of the wardrobe was a human being.

A man.

Or at least the skin of one.

The face, the skin covering the skull, and the rest of the body hung in the wardrobe, like an overcoat waiting to be put on. Gingerly Stimson touched the thing. It crackled to the touch as if alive with static electricity. Yet the skin seemed to be made of some soft, plastic material.

It was the skin of Klout the lawyer.

And yet it wasn't from any dead body. This skin had never covered a human being. It was merely an envelope. A disguise. But for what?

71

Stimson didn't wait to find out. He backed out of Klout's room and left the cabin immediately. He decided that he would rather face the Argolin than the creature that used that thing hanging in the wardrobe. He could not imagine what kind of creature it might be.

He was soon to find out.

Once in the lines between the cabins Stimson took to his heels, determined to put as much distance as he could between Brock's cabin and himself.

The creature saw him leave the cabin and pursued him swiftly on green, scaly feet. The creature ran down the corridor parallel to Stimson. It could see its prey between the cabins and tents. It moved faster than the Terran, and therefore entered the Great Recreation Hall before him.

It saw, wrapped around on the crystal statues of Argolin heroes, a long woollen object. It was the Doctor's scarf. It was ideal for its purpose. The creature took the scarf betwen two clawed hands and waited, poised behind a pillar.

As Stimson emerged into the Great Hall, the creature launched itself at him. It wrapped the scarf round the Terran's throat and pulled tighter and tighter. One bony knee was thrust into the small of Stimson's back. Desperately, with weakening fingers, the man tore at the scarf which was choking him.

The hourglass was placed in the centre of the six tachyon projectors. The sand was running from the upper vessel of the glass into the lower vessel.

'All right,' said Romana. 'Switch on.'

Hardin slowly fed the power into the projectors.

At first nothing happened. The projectors began to glow; the sand continued to run through the hourglass. But when power had built up sufficiently,

72

the hourglass was suddenly surrounded by a nimbus of light. Then a curious thing occurred. The sand began to flow more slowly through the neck of the glass. Until at last it fell into the vessel beneath grain by grain. Then it stopped. A few grains of sand were trapped halfway down, falling into the lower vessel. They floated as if riding on an invisible cloud.

'Perfect,' said Romana. 'Hold it there.'

'Stasis,' declared Hardin.

They both studied the phenomenon.

'Looks like it,' agreed Romana. 'You see what we've done is brought *that* time – the time within the hourglass – to a stop. That's all. The question is, can we turn back *that* time to the point where the sand was before it began to fall?'

'Let's try,' suggested Hardin.

So they did – and a circuit burned out.

'I don't understand,' complained Romana.

'Neither do I,' agreed Hardin. 'In theory this whole apparatus should function perfectly. Yet it doesn't. Why not?'

'There's only one way to find out, Hardin. Check back. Check it all over again. And then again – if it still doesn't work. That's one thing I've learned from the Doctor – when to check your facts and when to go on faith alone.

'Now,' she went on, 'is the time to check.'

The Doctor meanwhile had left Mena resting in the boardroom surrounded by Argolin medical orderlies. He had come down to the Great Recreation Hall, determined to investigate the generator while everyone else was occupied.

He studied the diagnostic display panel above the computer console and punched a few keys.

On the panel appeared the words: OVER-RIDE

FAIL SAFE. OVER-RIDE FAIL SAFE.

Then the words: ELIMINATE INTRUDER. ELIMINATE INTRUDER.

'So that's how it was done,' said the Doctor. 'Fascinating. And most ingenious. All pre-planned.'

'Doctor.'

The Doctor turned round to find that a group had gathered behind him – a group consisting of Pangol, Brock and various guides. They carried a stretcher on which lay the body of Stimson. Wound tightly round the Terran's throat, so tightly his eyes bulged out of their sockets, was the Doctor's scarf. Stimson had been strangled with the Doctor's scarf.

'This is your scarf, isn't it?' asked Pangol.

'Yes,' said the Doctor, 'for the umpteenth time it's my scarf. I've never denied that – not once over the past hour or so.'

They had long since moved back inside the boardroom, but in the course of time the atmosphere had deteriorated considerably. The Doctor was on trial, and the Argolin wanted blood. His, preferably.

'Do you deny that your scarf was the one that throttled Henrick Stimson to death?'

'No,' said the Doctor.

'It was found wrapped round the deceased's neck.'

'Then the scarf is guilty,' snapped the Doctor. 'Arrest it.'

No one was amused.

The Doctor looked round the cold, proud, intent faces of the Argolin who stood beside Mena. They gave the impression of waiting, ready, like good soldiers, to go out and do her bidding. The Doctor had the feeling that no matter what her orders they would obey. Without question, almost without thought. No wonder the Argolin had been the greatest warriors in the Galaxy. He glanced uneasily up at the great Helmet of Theron which dominated the boardroom, like an ancient curse.

'Let us go over the facts of the case once again,' said Mena in a feeble voice.

They had been working for several hours. Romana had checked every item of equipment and suggested various changed in the micro-circuitry. And now the experiment had reached a crucial phase. The sand in the hourglass hung in mid air: frozen. And yet, as Romana knew, each grain was still in motion, still falling but infinitely slowly. In the space within the hourglass, in the space bounded by the six tachyon projectors, time had been slowed to such a point that a second lasted for a day, an hour for nearly nine weeks.

'Ready?' asked Romana.

'Ready,' said Hardin.

In spite of all the improvements they had made he no longer had any confidence in the equipment. Many times in his experiments he had reached this point where it had seemed he was about to make the vital breakthrough. But at the very moment when he had been on the verge of mastering the flow of Time itself, something had always gone wrong.

'Start the recording now.'

Hardin switched on the recorder.

'I thought the Doctor was going to come down and help us,' he said.

'He was. I don't know where he's got to. I expect he'll turn up when all the hard work's been done.'

She studied the sand in the hourglass. 'Increase the power slowly,' she ordered. 'And stop when I tell you. A sudden surge might blow everything to pieces.'

Hardin called out the readings on the dials, waiting each time for the figures to stabilize themselves, and then gradually increasing the power flow. The sand in the hourglass remained static, frozen in the act of flowing into the lower vessel of the glass.

At one point Romana noticed a faint blurring of the grains of sand, almost a double image, as if for a fraction of a second there were two flows of sand attempting to occupy the same space.

'Hold it steady,' she called to Hardin while she checked the tachyon projectors.

When she looked again, the blurring had ceased. Each grain of sand hung poised in the throat of the glass, falling with infinite slowness.

Gradually Hardin built up the power.

'Reverse phase!' ordered Romana. 'Now!'

At first there was a slight flurry in the falling sand, as if someone was blowing upon it. Then something very strange occurred. The sand began to flow upwards. It was being sucked into the upper vessel of the glass.

Hardin and Romana watched the hourglass closely.

'We've done it,' he whispered. 'We've turned Time back on itself.'

'You see,' said Romana. 'Your theory's correct, your equipment works, your experiment is a success. And you haven't had to cheat.'

Hardin grinned. 'Let's go and tell Mena,' he said.

Laughing, they switched off the equipment and left the laboratory. Hardin paused at the door and looked back. The sand still remained in the upper vessel of the hourglass, unaffected by the normal laws of gravity.

'What's wrong?' asked Romana.

'Nothing,' he said. 'Not a thing.'

He closed the door behind them.

Ten minutes after they had gone something happened inside the hourglass. Gravity re-asserted itself: the sand suddenly flowed downwards into the lower vessel. In slow motion the upper part of the glass then buckled inwards. As the upper vessel imploded, the lower exploded, scattering sand and shards of glass over the laboratory.

The Doctor was annoyed – and, moreover, bored. Everyone knows the law is an ass. But Argolin justice seemed to have longer ears than most. Certainly it was quite remarkably tedious. As far as the Doctor could see, every Argolin had the right to offer comment, opinion or even actual evidence on the case in question. And it seemed to the Doctor that practically everyone on Argolis was eager to avail him or herself of the opportunity.

'Evidence?' snapped the Doctor irritably as an Argolin worthy offered some particularly tendentious peice of hearsay. 'You surely don't call that evidence, do you? Just a collection of uncorroborated rubbish. Purely circumstantial. Not enough to hang a hat on – let alone me.'

Mena reproved him. 'A murder has been committed,' she said.

'And the murderer found,' observed Brock.

'That has yet to be decided,' said Mena.

Pangol had a suggestion. 'In ancient times,' he announced, 'when the great Theron was alive, he threw a man into a fiery furnace or a lake, and let the elements decide his guilt or innocence.'

But the Doctor wasn't impressed. 'They used to do that on Earth once,' he declared. 'With witches. Didn't prove anything though – except that some women could swim better than others.

'However if you're absolutely set on that sort of

thing,' he added, 'there's an odd-looking blue box parked in the Great Recreation Hall. You could lock me and Romana in it – and see what happens. If it vanishes, we're innocent; if it doesn't we're guilty.'

But unfortunately no one seemed to be interested in the proposition.

By the time Romana and Hardin returned to the boardroom the Doctor's legal position was still no clearer. As owner of the scarf that had strangled Stimson, he still remained chief suspect. But since no one had seen him do the deed and since no one could offer a convincing motive as to why he should want to throttle the Terran to death, the case – such as it was – remained unproven.

Mena greeted the arrival of Romana and Hardin with some relief. Now the ageing process had begun she found it harder and harder to concentrate for any length of time on one subject.

'Romana's solved the wave equations for all four dimensions,' he declared.

Mena looked at him blankly.

'It means that the machine actually can reverse the time flow,' he explained. 'Which means that it can rejuvenate tissue. It could rejuvenate you.'

'Probably,' added Romana, aware that Hardin was making as yet unsubstantiated claims. After all they had not tested the machine with a living organism.

Mena found the whole idea difficult to grasp. 'I am dying,' she said. 'I know that. My metabolic rate has begun to speed up. Do you mean to say that you could stop the process?'

'Stop it?' cried Hardin. 'We could reverse it! Make you twenty, thirty years younger.'

'Possibly,' interjected Romana.

'Very possibly,' she added, 'after we've made a few tests with living organisms.'

Pangol laughed mirthlessly. 'You want to test a living organism,' he said. 'So do we.' He indicated the Doctor. 'What about him? Trial by ordeal. It's the ancient Argolin way.'

'You must have lost a lot of litigants over the years,' observed the Doctor.

'At least we don't need any court of appeal on Argolis.'

Much to Romana's horror, Mena and the assembled Argolin thought it the ideal solution. The Doctor would be the guinea-pig in Hardin's test.

'But there isn't room in the laboratory,' objected Hardin. 'The Doctor won't fit into an hourglass.'

'As I understand it,' said Pangol, 'all you need for your process to work are tachyon projectors. Right?'

Hardin nodded.

'Then use the recreation generator. There are twenty-five projectors incorporated into that.'

So it was decided that the Doctor would submit to trial in the generator.

The Doctor, however, was less than enthusiastic about the idea.

'Don't worry,' Romana told him.

'Well, not much,' she added. 'We know the technique works. But I doubt if it will take more than ten or twelve years off your age.'

'You're sure of that?' demanded the Doctor.

'No. But it's probably only a temporary effect anyway,' she replied. 'It's not likely you'll get total tissue regeneration.'

The Argolin were arguing the legal niceties of his case. The Doctor held up his hand. 'Am I correct in assuming that if I survive this ordeal by tachyon generator, then I am deemed to be innocent of the crime of which I am accused?' he asked.

79

'That is the legal position according to ancient Argolin law,' agreed Mena.

'Good,' said the Doctor. 'Then I volunteer for the test. Indeed, I insist upon it.' He extended his arms to the Argolin Security guides. 'Lead me to the generator.'

Romana took Hardin to one side. 'We ought to record this,' she remarked. 'You're needed here to make sure Pangol programmes the generator computer correctly. I'll go down to the laboratory and switch on the recorder.'

The Argolin had a talent for parades and processions – no doubt the result of their military tradition. They fell into formation around the Doctor, and in slow time, with everyone – except the Doctor – in step, marched down to the Great Hall.

At the door to the recreation generator the Doctor turned to make a speech to his Argolin audience. 'I am innocent of the murder of the Earthling,' he declared. 'The generator will prove it.' He bowed to his audience and shut the door of the generator behind him.

When Romana opened the door of the laboratory, an extraordinary sight met her eyes. The exploding lower vessel of the hourglass had been trapped in an expanding time bubble. The flying sand and shards of glass were frozen in mid air, trapped like flies in amber. They hung there as if caught by the lens of a camera. But when Romana wonderingly touched one of the particles of glass, it disintegrated into dust.

Realizing the significance of what had happened, she turned and ran from the room.

'Doctor!' she cried. 'Don't!'

But she was too late.

Pangol was already activating the recreation generator when Romana reached the Great Hall.

Lights were flashing on the control console. The bubble screen was filled with a kind of grey smoke.

Ignoring Pangol, Romana hit the stop button on the generator's console.

The screen went dark.

Romana tugged at the door of the generator. At last, with agonizing slowness, it opened.

'Doctor,' she cried, 'are you all right?'

7

Mirror, Mirror, on the Wall

'Yes,' said the Doctor. 'I think so. A bit out of breath, of course. And my legs feel strange.' He looked round the circle of anxious faces. 'What's wrong?' he demanded. 'Why are you looking at me like that?'

He put his hand to his face. The skin of his cheeks felt rough and hard. He looked at his hands. The fingers were gnarled and twisted, like oak twigs. The skin on the back of his hands was blotched with brown spots.

He had no mirror. But the exterior of the generator was covered in black, shiny glass. He turned and peered shortsightedly at his reflection.

A bent, wrinkled, white-haired figure stared back at him.

Who was it? It couldn't be him surely. But it was. A terrible caricature of himself stared back at him.

'Is that me?' he asked wonderingly.

'There must have been a hardware malfunction,' said Romana almost in tears.

'But I've got so old.' He continued to stare at his reflection. 'Why should it have this effect? It doesn't make sense.' He frowned desperately, trying to whip his failing memory into life. 'There was something I was going to check when I was in there.'

'What?' asked Romana.

'I can't remember,' he said.

Mena patted the Doctor's hand comfortingly.

'You're not well, Doctor,' she said. 'Go and lie down in one of the cabins.'

'He's still on trial for murder,' objected Pangol.

'I thought that was his trial!' snapped Romana. 'Trial by ordeal.'

'It was,' replied Pangol. 'And how would you describe the verdict?' He turned to the Security guides. 'Confine them both.'

The guides looked to Mena for confirmation. But she was leaning on Hardin's arm, gasping for breath. At last she nodded.

'Very well. I declare a limitation on them.'

With Romana holding one arm and a Security guide the other the Doctor shuffled slowly towards the cabins.

'What's a limitation?' he asked.

'A simple form of restraint,' explained the guide. 'Quite painless. Unless you do something stupid.'

The Doctor paused and cupped one hand to his ear. 'Eh?'

'Your movements are proscribed,' said the guide in a louder voice. 'Programmed. It's as if you were on a chain. Except there's no chain.'

The Doctor shook his head blankly. But he found out soon enough. Vargos was waiting for them in the cabin. He carried two ornate silver collars. One he clipped round Romana's neck; the other he fitted onto the Doctor's wrinkled throat.

'You'll find them quite comfortable to wear, so long as you keep within the limits ordained for you,' he explained. 'The collars are programmed to forbid you access to certain parts of the Leisure Hive. For example, you are forbidden to enter the Great Recreation Hall where your blue box stands or the laboratories or the boardroom or the shuttle station.

Otherwise you are free to roam where you like.'

'What happens if we go into a forbidden area?' demanded Romana.

'The collar will contract around your neck. It will squeeze tighter and tighter until it chokes you to death.'

There was a choking sound from the Doctor. They turned to find him tearing at his collar, his face contorted in agony.

'The collar also contracts if you attempt to remove it,' remarked Vargos. 'Take your hands away, Doctor.'

The Doctor obeyed and suddenly found he was no longer choking.

'It really is quite simple,' said Vargos. 'Behave yourself and you feel no discomfort. But put one foot outside your prescribed area and you will be unconscious within two minutes; dead in three.'

When Argolin had gone, the Doctor inspected his collar in the mirror. Gingerly he put up his hand to touch it, then stopped. He had caught sight of his own reflection. Good Lord, he thought, that old man is me. It was almost like a regeneration, where quite suddenly you experienced a total physical change. A new body, in fact. And when you first looked in the mirror, you didn't recognize yourself. He regarded his white hair and wrinkled skin with distaste. I don't recognize you, old man, he thought.

'Do you think I look twelve hundred and fifty?' he asked Romana, turning his head this way and that. His neck was as scrawny as an underfed chicken's.

'Be honest,' he said.

'You don't look a day over a thousand,' she replied lightly.

But the Doctor was in no mood for pleasantries. 'We've got to do something. And soon. Because I don't know how long I've got. It's difficult to work out the life-expectancy of a Time Lord in any one body. Still, if looks are anything to go by, I'll be lucky to see the week out in this one.'

'If only we could get you back into the generator and reverse the process.'

'Brilliant,' said the Doctor sourly. 'To get near the generator we've got to get out of these collars first. How do we do that?'

Romana didn't reply. Gently, using one finger, she touched her collar and immediately felt it contract round her neck. No, it wasn't going to be easy.

Brock meanwhile had been investigating the situation at the shuttle service desk. He had been watching queues of holidaymakers trying to get a seat.

'Its a mass exodus,' he reported back to Mena. 'Everyone's leaving, or trying to. And I can't say I blame them. There have been two murders and a nasty accident in one day. It's enough to put anyone off their holiday. And mark my words, once the visitors leave here they'll never come back.'

'I think you may be exaggerating—'

'Do you? Take a look.' Brock switched on the boardroom video screens.

A milling crowd of holidaymakers could be seen fighting for places in the queue for shuttle tickets. There was an air of barely repressed hysteria about the scene.

'Rats leaving a sinking ship. Not,' he went on, 'that I'm criticizing rats. If a ship is sinking, it makes good sense to get off it. And if there is a murderer loose on Argolis, why hang around and run the risk of becoming Victim Number Three?'

'What can we do?' asked Mena.

'Sell Argolis now before the Foamasi get to hear about all this.'

Mena shook her head.

'Sell,' pleaded Brock. 'All you have to do is to sign the contract. Let the Foamasi sort out the problems.'

Mena pointed to the video screen. 'If only we could find some way of restoring their confidence in the Leisure Hive,' she said.

'Give them justice,' suggested Pangol. 'A public trial followed by a public execution. We have caught the murderers. We have them under limitation. Let the vsitors see them pay for their crimes with their lives.'

'The Doctor and Romana?' Mena stared at Pangol in horror. 'But he survived trial by ordeal. And we have no evidence at all against her.'

He pointed to the struggling mass of holiday-makers. 'They don't care about evidence. What they want is instant justice. Then the rats will feel safe.

'In any case,' he went on, 'who's going to miss an alien Doctor from some tinpot planet?'

When Hardin entered the cabin where the Doctor and Romana were, he found the former trying to remove his limitation collar.

'Try this key,' said Hardin. 'I borrowed it from the Security Office while all the guides were busy trying to control the crowds round the shuttle desk.'

He quickly released the other two from their collars.

'Look,' he explained. 'I need your help. I think we could save Mena – stop the cellular degeneration – if we can use the full power of the generator—'

'Ever thought why they call it that?' remarked the Doctor sitting up with some difficulty.

'What?'

'The generator. The recreation generator.'

Hardin looked at the aged, white-haired figure squatting on the floor. Better humour the old chap, he thought.

'No,' he replied kindly. 'Why do they call it that?'

'Re-creation.'

'Re-creation?' repeated Hardin. He looked for elucidation to Romana. She shrugged.

'It means creating things anew.'

'What things?'

'New things,' said the Doctor vaguely. 'New creations.'

Hardin nodded. Humour him, he thought. Poor old fellow, his brain's gone.

'It doesn't matter,' said the Doctor. 'Just bear the thought in mind.'

So this is what it's like being old, he reflected. Everyone thinks you are a candidate for the funny farm just because you have a few white hairs and are a bit forgetful now and again.

Brock was pushing to close the deal with Mena. Her strength was failing fast, but she was Heresiarch of Argolis, and as such her agreement was required before the contract could be signed. She peered at the document, desperately trying to concentrate.

'The Foamasi are offering excellent terms,' he declared. 'Considering that as a Leisure Planet Argolis isn't exactly amongst the top money-spinners in the galaxy.'

'It means the end of our planet.'

'Which is finished anyway.'

'The Foamasi expect us to pack our bags and become galactic gypsies?'

'*Rich* galactic gypsies, Mena.'

'Suppose we stay?'

Brock sighed and shook his head. 'Don't you understand?' he said. 'You don't have that kind of choice. In a few months' time you'll be faced with the same problem. You'll still have to leave because the Hive is crumbling and you can't afford to repair it. What's more, you won't have thirty trillion galactic credits to cushion the shock.'

'There is an alternative,' said Mena. 'When the day comes, we can open the airlocks, and together the last of the Argolin will walk out onto the surface of our planet for the last time.'

Brock stared at her incredulously. 'You mean you'd all rather commit suicide than go off and live on some other planet. I don't understand you people. Tell me, what is so special about this place? The atmosphere's poisonous; the landscape's just sand and cinders, and not much of that. What is the attraction?'

'This is Argolis,' replied Mena.

Meanwhile Pangol had been studying the contract. It was stamped with a curious seal consisting of interlocking hexagons.

'This isn't an official Foamasi Government document!' he announced.

'Did I say it was?' demanded Brock. 'If you must know, this is a private deal. The offer is being made by a group of concerned Foamasi business creatures.'

Pangol pointed out the name on the contract. 'The West Lodge?'

Brock nodded. 'That is the title of their organization. Does it matter what they call themselves?'

But Pangol still wasn't satisfied. 'What do they propose to do with our planet?' He flourished the document. 'They don't explain that here.'

'They don't have to, Pangol. That's because what

you're holding is a contract to purchase – not an application for building permission. And don't ask me what they propose to build either,' continued Brock. 'Because I don't know.'

He drew a deep breath. Don't get angry, he told himself. Keep your temper. It's just Pangol behaving like a typical Argolin.

'Look,' he said. 'Let's be honest. Forgetting suicide for the moment, you have two choices as I see it – bankruptcy or the Foamasi. In your position I know which I'd choose.'

'There is another way,' declared Pangol. 'We can build the new Argolis.'

The corridor between the cabins was clear. There was no one about. The holidaymakers were all in the First Observation Hall, while all available Security guides were trying to preserve some semblance of order. It wasn't easy.

No one therefore raised the alarm when Hardin and the two prisoners emerged from the cabin. Hardin and Romana each took the Doctor by an arm and helped him down the corridor.

He suddenly paused.

'Where are we going?'

'To the generator,' said Romana.

'It was your idea, Doctor,' said Hardin.

The Doctor nodded and tried to look as if he knew what he planned to do once he got there. The truth was he didn't. He recalled that he had had some plan back there in the cabin. But what it was he couldn't for the life of him remember.

'Don't worry,' he told the others. 'It'll come back to me.'

Brock was unimpressed by Pangol's rhetoric. 'The

new Argolis,' he sneered. 'What's that?'

'It is waiting to be born.'

'I'm delighted to hear it,' declared the Terran. 'I hope you'll call me when it happens. In fact, I wouldn't miss it for the worlds – because it will need a real miracle to bring it about.

'Forgive me for reminding all you nice people,' he went on, 'but this is a sterile planet. You are a sterile race. There hasn't been an Argolin born here, or anywhere else for that matter, since the War. And that was forty years ago.'

'You're wrong, Mr Brock.'

'About the War?'

Pangol smiled. 'I'm not over forty,' he said. 'I'm twenty-five. How do you explain that?'

Night on Argolis was perhaps even more spectacular than the day. At night the 'jewels of Argolis', as some long-forgotten poet had christened them – the seven Argolin moons – reflected light from the suns. The rainbow-hued atmosphere of the planet, the ever-changing kaleidoscope of colours, was transmuted into tones of blue and silver and grey as the moonlight was refracted by the dust clouds.

Argolis, thought Romana, was one of the most beautiful planets she had ever seen, particularly if you saw it from behind glass. She, Hardin and the Doctor had paused in the shadow of the wall of the Great Recreation Hall, and she was staring upwards through the dome at the night sky. The Doctor meanwhile was leaning against the wall panting for breath. He was discovering that adventure was hard on the lungs and the knees at his age. The other two waited for him to recover.

'In a minute,' he gasped. 'Just give me a minute. I'll be all right.'

90

They waited.

'Facts,' he said at last. 'Fact: the Argolin have devoted years to research and vast sums of money they can ill afford to the study of tachyonics. Yet apparently all they have got out of it is a cabinet of illusions, which may be ingenious but is hardly worth all that expenditure.'

They nodded.

'Fact: the Argolin are sterile. Fact: there are no children on Argolis.'

He stood gasping for breath, like a fish out of water.

'Well?' demanded Romana. 'What's your conclusion?'

The Doctor shook his head. 'I can't remember,' he confessed. 'I've forgotten.' Then his eyes lit up. 'No, I haven't. The tachyon recreation generator must represent some attempt on the part of the Argolin to solve their population problem.'

But Romana remained unconvinced. 'A machine won't give them children. No machine can create life from scratch.'

'You're forgetting the significance of the name.'

'What name?' asked Romana.

'Recreation?' suggested Hardin.

'Right,' agreed the Doctor. 'The recreation generator. It must have some capacity for cellular reduplication.'

'Cloning?'

'No. The tachyon particle is too unstable.'

'Then what?'

The Doctor sighed and closed his eyes. 'I don't know,' he said at last. 'I've forgotten.' He sounded weary. The effort of concentration had proved too much for him.

'We had better find out then,' she said.

Hardin volunteered for the task of going into the generator, and Romana was tempted to let him do it. But she knew that in the end there was only one of them who could afford the risk.

'It has to be me,' she said. 'Unfortunately.'

'Why?' asked Hardin.

'Because the Doctor's too—'

'Say it,' snapped the Doctor. 'Too old!'

'If there's another tachyon surge while you're inside, you'd never survive it.'

The Doctor mumbled grumpily to himself, but he did not contradict her.

'What about me?' demanded Hardin.

'You're a Terran.'

'What's that got to do with it?'

'Because you've only a limited life span. You can't afford to age five hundred years in a few minutes.'

'Can you?' asked Hardin.

'Yes,' said Romana. 'Unfortunately.'

What will I look like when I'm 650, she wondered? Unconsciously she stroked her long blonde hair. Will it go white? Will I be bald?

The Doctor pointed to the generator. 'Guards,' he said. They looked round and saw that two Argolin Security guides had taken up positions by the generator.

Brock was confused. He looked to Mena for assistance. 'I don't understand,' he said. 'If the Argolin have been sterile for forty years, yet Pangol's only twenty-five....

'Isn't he a pure Argolin?' he asked.

Pangol laughed. 'I'm the purest Argolin of them all,' he declared.

Brock again appealed to Mena. 'Was he adopted?' But she did not reply.

'I always thought he was your child, yours and Morix's.'

Mena would not meet his eyes.

'I am the first of the new Argolin,' declared Pangol proudly. He drew himself to his full height. 'I am the Child of the Generator.'

The two Security guides were obviously on duty for the next few hours. They did not move from the generator.

'What we need,' said Hardin, 'is a diversion.'

The Doctor, who had been showing signs of dozing off whilst leaning against the wall, suddenly jerked awake. 'Did I ever tell you what I thought the generator was really designed for?' he asked.

'You couldn't remember,' said Romana.

'Oh.'

The Doctor closed his eyes and began to snore.

Just at that moment two Science guides appeared. Their job was to carry out daily maintenance on the generator.

'That does it,' said Romana, not without a certain relief in her voice. 'I'll never get past the four of them.'

The Doctor woke up. 'What we need,' he said, 'is a diversion. Come on.'

And before the others could stop him he started to walk across to the maintenance crew. He waved to them. 'Hello,' he called. 'Could I have a word?'

'He's gone mad,' whispered Hardin. 'He must have done. Senile dementia, that's what it is. It affects people when they get old.'

They watched the Doctor's rather arthritic progress across the Great Recreation Hall.

'What's he going to do?'

'Heaven knows,' replied Romana. 'But no matter what it is – come on!'

Together she and the Terran scientist began to make their way, unseen, towards the generator.

The Security guides observed the Doctor's slow approach with some suspicion. Obviously he was no longer under official limitation, otherwise he would have worn a programmed collar. Nevertheless it didn't pay to get careless. They decided to keep an eye on him.

The two-man maintenance crew were busy running a routine computer check. The Doctor paused to chat to them. The Security guides could not hear what he was saying, but one of the men shook his head and pointed to the computer. The Doctor took a piece of chalk out of his pocket and began to scrawl equations on the top of the control console. The maintenance men studied them, scratched their heads and began to argue with him.

Meanwhile at Romana's urging, Hardin emerged from the shadows and began to stroll across the Great Hall in the direction of the generator.

Approached from two different directions at once the Security guides were distracted. When one of the maintenance men suddenly moaned and collapsed onto the floor, they left their posts and came over to see if they could help.

'Poor chap,' said the Doctor sympathetically. 'I tried to introduce him to the computer language they use on Hermes-4a. Must have been too much for him. Overheated his brain, I expect.'

While the Security guides were trying to revive the unconscious maintenance man, Romana was able to slip unobserved inside the generator.

Pangol smiled at Brock. His eyes glittered like chips of glass. 'I think it's time, my fat Terran friend,' he said, 'that you learned something of the forbidden

94

secrets of the Argolin.'

He put an arm round the accountant's broad shoulders. Surprised at the unexpected physical contact with someone from a race as noted for their reserve as the Argolin were, Brock recoiled. Pangol laughed. 'Don't worry, my friend,' he continued, 'you won't be expected to undergo any painful initiation ceremonies.'

'Pangol, is this wise?' asked Mena.

Pangol ignored her.

'After the Foamasi War,' he said, 'the Argolin knew they were doomed to extinction within a generation. Unless they could find some other way of reproducing themselves. As you know, virtually the only Argolin survivors of the War were all members of the crew of Morix's hyperspace war galley.'

'I was communications officer,' said Mena.

'The scientific officer aboard *The Rage of Theron* – that was the name of Morix's ship – was called Verdrix,' went on Pangol. 'He devoted himself to the problem of the survival of our race. His answer was the generator.'

'What happened to him?' asked Brock.

'He died,' replied Mena. 'He was the first of the Argolin to age.'

'But he had completed the generator,' said Pangol. 'So twenty-six years ago the Argolin were at last ready for the great experiment.'

Mena spoke. Her voice was feeble but clear. Her eyes looked inwards, fixed only on the past. 'None of us will ever forget that day. For the first time it seemed as if a great dark cloud was lifting from us. It seemed as if once again the voice of our young would be heard on Argolis.'

'The Argolin,' explained Pangol, 'and there were many more of them then than there are today, the

Argolin donated living cells from their own bodies. Thousands of cells. They placed them in the generator. The aim was to clone them. The cloned cells would then be incubated, fed on nutrients, until they became embryos and ultimately foetuses.'

Brock looked puzzled. 'Where are these clones?' he asked. 'What happened to them?'

Pangol did not reply at first. Then he said: 'The tachyon is an inherently unstable particle. At that time no one realized how unstable it was.'

'What about the cloning?' demanded Brock.

'There were many failures.'

'I don't understand.' Brock turned to Mena. 'What does he mean?'

Mena sighed. 'Poor, dead, disfigured creatures.'

'Mutants most of them, I imagine,' said Pangol. 'Few survived birth. Those that did were usually better off dead.'

'What about you, Pangol?'

'I was the sole survivor,' replied the young Argolin. 'The generator made me. The generator gave birth to me. I am the Child of the Generator.'

As he spoke, he switched the boardroom video screens to the Great Recreation Hall. All cameras covered the shining black bulk of the generator. One of them picked up an all-too-familiar figure. Bent, white haired, the Doctor could be seen at the computer control console.

Pangol reacted immediately.

'What's he doing there?' he cried. He pressed the alarm button and ran from the boardroom.

When the alarm sounded in the Great Recreation Hall, Hardin half dragged the Doctor away from the generator.

'But Romana's in there,' protested the Doctor.

'If the Argolin see us hanging around, they'll figure that out for themselves,' snapped Hardin.

Whether it was the logic of his argument or the fact that for one terrible moment he could not remember who Romana was, the Doctor allowed Hardin to lead him over to the elevator which took them down to the laboratory. It was fortunate that he did so – because just as the elevator doors closed behind them, Pangol, followed by a group of Security guides, entered the Hall.

On the order from Pangol the guides split up to search every corner of the Great Hall. 'Find them!' he cried. 'The Doctor. The girl. Hardin. I want them found.'

Afraid that the Doctor might have sabotaged the computer of the generator, Pangol went over to check it for himself. He punched out his instructions. On the diagnostic panel flashed the words: SECURITY. STATUS UP-DATE.

Pangol waited. 'Did you see anyone go into the generator?' he asked the maintenance man.

'No, sir.'

'All the same someone did get inside.' He pointed to the panel. On it appeared the words: INTRUDERS. INTRUDERS. INTRUDERS.

Some of the Security guides were about to open the door of the generator, when Pangol stopped them.

'I know who's in there,' he said. 'It seems a pity to disturb him. No, let him have his fun. And I think we ought to have a little, too.'

Pangol busied himself adjusting the various settings on the generator. In spite of what had happened to him the last time he had entered the generator, when he had emerged five hundred years older, the Doctor had gone back inside. He had survived his first visit. But Pangol determined to make quite sure that he wouldn't survive his second. Pangol doubted if even the Doctor's remarkable constitution could withstand ageing a further two thousand years. Still they would soon see.

Pangol switched on the power supply. He pressed the start button and felt the generator surge into life.

As it happened, at that moment the Doctor was sitting on a stool in the laboratory, trying to get his breath back. 'There's no doubt about,' he panted. 'All this rushing about takes it out of you when you get to be twelve hundred or so.'

'Do you think Romana's all right?' asked Hardin.

'She knows what she's doing,' replied the Doctor. 'At least I hope she does. Anyway, if she doesn't, she'll make a very attractive old lady.'

The door of the laboratory slid noiselessly open. There was a curious clicking noise behind them. The Doctor and Hardin leapt to their feet in alarm at the creature that entered.

It was something like a Terran lizard in shape, but tall as a man and covered with dark green scales. Two clawed hands gesticulated frantically, while from the throat of the creature came a succession of clicking and whistling noises.

'What the devil is it?' demanded Hardin.

'I don't know,' replied Romana, emerging from behind the creature and closing the door behind her. 'But at least he's a friend. He just saved my life. He got me out of the generator just before Pangol started it up.'

The Doctor frowned. 'You mean he was already in the image chamber of the generator when you got inside?'

Romana nodded.

'I wonder what our friend was doing there,' he mused.

The creature began to make a succession of whistling and clicking noises.

'Is he in pain?' asked Romana.

'I think he's just trying to communicate.'

'Where's he from?' demanded Hardin. 'What is he?'

'I don't care what he is,' declared Romana, patting a scaly shoulder. 'He saved my life, or at least saved me from becoming a very old lady.' She produced a small object which she handed to the Doctor. 'And he found that in the Image Chamber behind the second baryon shield.'

The creature whistled and clicked and gesticulated while the Doctor inspected the object. It turned out to be a transparent box containing a complex of slim gold leaves with a mirror on one side. The Doctor studies the box for some time. Then he handed it back to Romana. 'What is it?' he asked.

'A cell duplicator, of course,' she said. 'You ought to know that.'

'Yes,' replied the Doctor. 'Of course I should.' He sighed. 'It's just that I forget lately.'

The creature seized the Doctor by the arm and drew him over to the video screen. He pointed to the screen and then to the Doctor.

'I wish I knew what you wanted, my friend,' said the Doctor.

'Perhaps he wants to show us something on the screen,' suggested Hardin.

He switched on the video screen.

But the shots of the Great Recreation Hall were obviously not what the creature wanted. He whistled and clicked briefly and shook his head.

It was only when Hardin switched them through to the boardroom that the creature broke into a cacophany of clicks and whistles. He kept pointing to the screen. Pangol and Brock could be seen arguing, while Mena lay back weakly in her chair.

'Maybe he wants to talk to Mena,' said Romana.

The Doctor shook his head. 'It beats me,' he said.

Obviously despairing of making himself understood, the creature took the Doctor by the hand and pulled him towards the door.

'Come on!' cried the Doctor.

'Where to?' asked Hardin.

'Ask our scaly friend.'

The creature led the Doctor out of the laboratory, along the corridor and into the elevator. The other two followed closely on his heels. The creature took the elevator up three levels and then led them down another corridor.

'This leads to the boardroom,' complained Hardin.

The Doctor nodded. He was too out of breath to speak.

Hardin held Romana back for a moment. 'Are you sure this is a good idea?' he whispered. 'How do you know we can trust this lizard?'

'He saved my life,' said Romana. 'That's good enough for me.'

'Did he?'

'What do you mean?'

'Well, you don't actually know what he was doing in the Image Chamber of the generator in the first place. Do you?'

Before Romana could formulate a reply the creature flung open the boardroom door.

Pangol and Brock looked up, startled

The creature moved with extraordinary speed. Before anyone else had time to react he launched himself into the attack. He seized the Terran accountant, grappled him to the floor, and – to everyone's horror - forced one claw-like hand down his throat.

Brock's screams were swiftly stifled.

8

The Foamasi

The whole attack was so swift, so merciless, that no one had a chance to go to Brock's aid. Nor was anyone prepared for what happened next.

With a triumphant cacophany of whistles and clicks the creature held something aloft. Something small and oval in shape. Something he had removed from Brock's throat. Something which he proceeded to swallow himself.

The whistles and clicks suddenly died.

A voice said: 'Now at last I can speak to you.'

It was the creature.

Romana knelt beside the Terran accountant, who lay half-unconscious on the floor. 'Are you all right?' she asked.

His lips moved, but no words came.

'Mr Brock.'

Then something very strange happened. When Brock tried to speak, all that emerged was a series of whistles and clicks.

'It's all done by voice synthesizer,' explained the creature. 'Without his, our friend here cannot make himself understood.'

Mena sounded bewildered. 'Are you saying that Mr Brock has some sort of speech defect?' she asked.

'This isn't the real Brock,' replied the creature. With one knee on the chest of the recumbent Terran, he was tugging at the skin at the base of the neck. 'You'll find that the real Brock is alive and well and still living on Terra. In fact, he never left there.'

'But that's impossible.'

'Check, if you don't believe me.'

'I don't understand,' protested Mena. 'We've had dealings with Brock for the past ten years. I tell you that is him.'

There was a tearing sound.

'This,' said the creature, 'is the real face of the thing that you thought was Brock.'

With a gesture the creature ripped away the face of the accountant. The face came away like a mask. Underneath they could see green scaly skin and the features of something that resembled a lizard.

'These flesh suits are amazing. Accurate to a micron. Believe me, even Brock's own mother wouldn't have been able to tell the difference between the real man and what inhabited this suit!'

The creature deftly skinned the recumbent figure, removing the humanoid envelope that had formed such an impenetrable disguise for the green scaly creature beneath.

'On my planet flesh suits were banned years ago,' observed the creature. He fastened the false Brock's claw-like hands together with what looked like a strip of double-sided adhesive tape. 'Of course, there are still craftsmen who, for a price, will make one of these suits for you. But you will have to pay through the nose for it.'

Casually he rolled up the Brock skin, like a pair of old overalls.

Romana touched the skin. It still felt warm and soft as if it were made from incredibly fine suede.

'Originally these suits were designed for the professional assassins' market,' he went on. 'The idea was that, dressed in the guise of your victim's mother or best friend or even wife, the assassin could get close enough to make the kill. Our guild of assassins were furious when the Government banned these suits.

'That was in the bad old days,' he added.

'What planet?' asked the Doctor. 'What Government?'

The creature produced a small circular plaque. 'Those are my credentials,' he said. 'I am an agent from the Foamasi Bureau of Investigation.'

'Foamasi!' cried Pangol. 'You mean that you are a Foamasi?' He clenched his fists and glared at the creature. 'Your race destroyed this planet,' he shouted furiously.

'Your race destroyed my planet,' snapped the Foamasi agent.

For a moment it looked as if the two might continue the war there and then.

Romana attempted to defuse the situation. She was also curious. She asked Pangol. 'Didn't you know he was a Foamasi?'

'Of course not,' he replied. 'I never saw one before.'

She turned to the Foamasi agent. 'What about you?'

He shrugged his narrow shoulders. 'No Foamasi ever met an Argolin before.'

Even though she was an experienced Time traveller and had journeyed vast distances through Time and Space, Romana found it difficult to absorb the information. 'Do you mean to say,' she enquired, 'that the Argolin and the Foamasi virtually wiped each other out and yet they never even met? They never saw each other face to face?'

'Why should they?' demanded Pangol. 'What do you expect in time of war – a gilt-edged invitation? An official introduction? Shake hands and come out fighting? The great Theron taught us that victory goes to him who is the swiftest and the most ruthless.'

'Shoot first and ask questions afterwards. Is that it?' she said.

Pangol folded his arms across his chest and refused to reply.

'I think it's pathetic!' declared Romana.

The Doctor found old wars a boring and sometimes dangerous subject for conversation. 'What happened to the Foamasi?' he asked, changing the subject.

The agent explained that after the Argolin War ('We call it the Foamasi War,' snapped Pangol) few of his race were left alive. Moreover, due to a cruel trick of Fate, most of those who did survive were criminals imprisoned in the largest underground prison on Foamas.

'So we were left,' he continued, 'with the remains of a society which was split between law and order on the one hand – represented by the surviving prison officers – and the criminals on the other. They came to be known as the White and the Black Foamasi.'

He went on to tell them how the Whites, though fewer in number, were more united than the Blacks, who were constantly rent by internal disputes. All the great Foamasi criminal clans, or 'families' as they were called, were represented amongst the survivors. In the past the clans had always devoted much of their time trying to eliminate their rivals. Their surviving brethren therefore continued the tradition. Ancient vendettas were pursued; old scores were settled; clan fought clan even more savagely than before. In time the clans themselves fragmented. They split up into smaller and smaller units, and thus could be picked off by the White Foamasi.

Some years ago the Foamasi Bureau of Investigation had been formed, with the object of breaking the power of the surviving clans – of which only two remained – the Twin Suns and the West Lodge.

'This contract carries the West Lodge crest,' said Mena.

'So does our friend,' observed the creature, turning the false Brock round so that everyone could see the design of interlocking hexagrams tattooed on his shoulder.

'He wanted to buy our planet,' declared Pangol.

The creature nodded. 'That's their usual approach. The West Lodge have been buying several planets lately.'

'What's wrong with buying planets?' asked Romana.

'Nothing,' agreed the agent. 'Providing purchaser and vendor agree a price. And providing the sale is according to galactic law. But the curious thing is that the West Lodge have never had to complete a contract yet.'

'What do you mean?'

It seemed that the West Lodge's purchases always followed the same pattern. Once they had located a suitable planet, they began discreet negotiations. If in the course of these they met any opposition, their opponents were apt to die in mysterious circumstances. There would also be a sudden spate of accidents. Power surges, computer failures, minor epidemics, defences against natural disasters unaccountably breached. Never any major calamities, but just enough to persuade the vendor that his planet was a less than desirable place to live.

With a great show of good faith the West Lodge would then make the first down-payment. Often a very generous sum. Say, three trillion galactic credits. Which the by now disillusioned and often desperate population would eagerly accept. Then, just as the second payment fell due, the planet would suffer some major catastrophe, like a multiple comet strike or a space-born plague. It was never the same catastrophe: on each occasion a different disaster would befall. But whatever it was it wiped out the population.

Since they had made the down-payment in good faith and since it was demonstrably no fault of theirs that they were unable to complete the contract, under galactic law the West Lodge were entitled to claim the planet. Purchase by default, it was called.

'All legal and above board.'

'I don't think I would call murdering the entire population of a planet legal,' observed the Doctor.

'Neither would I,' agreed the creature. 'But apparently the computer which drew up the law never considered that possibility. Probably it had never heard of the Black Foamasi.'

'Do you mean that is what this creature' – Mena pointed to the false Brock – 'would have done here?'

'Why should they treat Argolis differently from any other planet?' asked the Foamasi agent. 'I believe you had already had some accidents and sudden deaths. And you would have had more. Until no holidaymaker in his senses would want to come here at all. The offer from the West Lodge would still be on the table, and by now it would begin to look more and more generous. You would receive the down-payment – and that would be the last of the Argolin.'

Mena looked round the boardroom. 'Where's Klout?' she asked. 'I haven't seen him lately.'

'Klout?'

She pointed to the false Brock. 'His assistant. A lawyer. He never seemed to talk.'

'Couldn't, I expect,' remarked the Foamasi.

'Without giving himself away. Probably didn't have a voice synthesizer. Anyway he wouldn't need it. Klout will have been the sabotage expert and assassin. The West Lodge usually start by sending in a two-man team. The heavy brigade move in later.

'I'll order my men to find him.'

From under one of the large scales on his chest he took what looked like a tiny bone flute. He put it to his lips and blew a note. It made no sound.

'Ultra high frequency sound,' he explained, replacing the flute. 'Only Foamasi can hear it.'

At the sound of the flute call the other Foamasi agents began their search for Klout. The flute had told them where to look. Klout was the sabotage expert. He would be found in that part of the Leisure Hive where his expertise would do most damage – in the corridors below the Great Recreation Hall, in the service areas where the main power lines, communication channels, and life-support systems were located.

Two of the agents caught him red-handed. He was in the act of placing a small explosive charge in the air-purification plant. Challenged to halt in the high-pitched series of whistles and clicks that composed the present Foamasi language, Klout acted swiftly. He threw the limpet grenade at the agents. Fortunately he had not yet primed the grenade, which therefore bounced harmlessly off the wall beside them.

The grenade distracted them long enough for him to draw his electric stiletto. But, before he could strike, one of the agents lobbed something that resembled a ball of white wool at him. The moment the wool touched Klout it unravelled, wrapping him in a tight white cocoon, like a butterfly or moth larva. Struggle as he might, Klout could not move a muscle.

The two agents carried the cocooned Foamasi up to the boardroom, where they found their superior in collision with Pangol.

Pangol was demanding that, since the false Brock and his henchmen had broken Argolin law, they should stand trial on Argolis. However, the senior Foamasi agent insisted that galactic law, not to mention Foamasi law, took precedence under the circumstances. As he pointed out, it was not until he had unmasked Brock that the Argolin were even aware that they had welcomed an impostor into their midst. Certainly they could try the criminals after they had served their sentences on one of the penal satellites of Foamas.

Mena was not disposed to argue the point. 'Let him have the two criminals,' she told Pangol. 'So long as they stand trial somewhere, what does it matter where?'

Romana and the Doctor accompanied the Foamasi to the shuttle bay.

'I must confess I was worried about the Argolin reaction to us,' remarked the senior agent, as they walked down the corridor. 'In view of our past history I was afraid we might meet a lot of opposition here. I am relieved it has all ended so satisfactorily.'

'If it has ended,' observed the Doctor.

'Oh, I assure you that with the arrest of these two miscreants, Argolis will be in no more danger.'

'I wasn't thinking of Argolis.'

The senior agent paused. 'You think there might still be trouble?' he asked.

'Let's not cross any bridges until they're hatched,' replied the Doctor.

In the boardroom he would have found his worst fears confirmed.

Pangol was insisting that the aliens must not be allowed to leave Argolis.

'Why ever not?' asked Mena.

'They are spies.'

Mena wondered if the shock of meeting the Argolin's historic enemy for the first time had not been too much for Pangol. He was after all the only child of the Argolin. He had been brought up alone, without friends or confidants of his own age, amidst a dying population. It was not surprising therefore that he had become slightly paranoid.

The extent of his paranoia was to become clear only later.

Mena appealed to his reason. 'They are Government agents,' she said. 'You saw their credentials; you heard what they said.'

'You mean you actually believed all that claptrap?' sneered Pangol.

'Why should they lie?'

'Didn't it occur to you that theirs was just the sort of story you would invent if you wanted to provide a cover for your real purpose?'

'What purpose?' she demanded.

'The infiltration of Argolis.'

Pangol began to pace up and down the room, like a caged beast.

'It is perfectly clear,' he said. 'Those agents must have been sent ahead of the main Foamasi force to report on our defences. They broke into the Hive, and they have had every opportunity to discover our weaknesses. Once they report back to their Government it is only a matter of time before the Foamasi launch another full scale war.'

'But why?' she asked. 'Even if what you say were true, it must be obvious to the Foamasi that we constitute no threat to them.'

110

'Order the Foamasi to be detained!' Pangol commanded.

Mena summoned all her strength. She tried to rise to her feet, but the effort was too much for her. 'I am Heresiarch,' she said weakly. 'I decide the future of Argolis – not you. In this I will be obeyed.'

Pangol looked round the faces of the other Argolin, then he stepped forward and took down the Helmet of Theron from where it hung on the wall.

'Your time is over, old woman,' he said.

He placed the blackened duelling helmet on his head.

'All decisions are now in the hands of the great Theron.'

'No!' cried Mena. 'You must not wear the Helmet!'

'It is the symbol of Argolin power.'

'Theron worshipped war. It was through him that eventually we were reduced to the sterile, ageing creatures we are today.'

Pangol looked down on her, his eyes glittering strangely through the eyeholes in the helmet.

'We, Pangol, Child of the Generator, will fulfil Theron's dream of conquest.'

'How can you?' she asked, trying to reason with him. 'We have no army.' She turned pleadingly to the other Argolin. 'This is madness.'

Pangol spoke, his words echoing oddly from within the helmet: 'We, Pangol, will provide the greatest army Argolis has ever seen.'

The significance of his words dawned on her. She stared at him in horror. 'Do you mean that you have found a way to use the generator to....No, Pangol, I beg you—'

Ignoring her, Pangol turned to the other Argolin. 'Do you obey the great Theron?'

111

Old habits die hard. From forty years past the old Argolin military ethic reasserted itself. It was as if all those years of being polite to holidaymakers, of being the faceless servants to alien visitors, had fallen away. The iron discipline that had made the Argolin so feared throughout the galaxy gripped them and held them fast.

'An Argolin knight never refuses an order,' declared the Tenth Precept of Theron.

'An Argolin knight obeys his leader without question,' runs the Eleventh.

'To die gloriously in battle against the enemies of Argolis is the greatest joy an Argolin knight can hope to experience,' runs the Last Precept.

Vargos and the other Argolin, almost against their will, found themselves making the ancient salute which acknowledges fealty in time of war: they struck their left breast with their clenched right fist.

When she saw that, Mena knew she had lost.

The first sign the Doctor and the Foamasi had that the situation had changed was when the automatic doors leading to the shuttle bays suddenly closed in their faces.

'What's happening?' demanded the Foamasi agent.

'I don't know,' replied the Doctor.

Romana nudged him. 'I have a nasty feeling—' she said.

'We came to Argolis in peace,' protested the Foamasi. 'We came to save them from the depredations of some of our own criminals. It was a simple police action.'

'I'd keep trying to get that door open,' advised the Doctor. 'We'll go and see what the Argolin are up to.'

'Tell them that under galactic law we have full diplomatic immunity,' declared the Foamasi. 'Should anything happen to us my Government may feel duty bound to take military action.'

The Doctor nodded. 'Use your shoulders,' he suggested. 'Put everything into it. You might manage to get the doors open.'

Romana and the Doctor got to the Great Recreation Hall in time to see Pangol's entrance. He wore the Helmet of Theron and was followed by a procession of Argolin guides. They moved like zombies, ageing knights hypnotized by ghosts from the past. It was as if the great Theron once more commanded their lives.

Pangol paused and stretched wide his arms as if to encompass the extraordinary vista visible through the glass of the dome.

'Wait!' he cried. 'There is the Argolin dawn.'

Gradually a deep red sunrise of spectacular luminosity, lit here and there by green flashes of light, spread across the sky.

'It is the Dawn of the New Argolis.'

As the twin suns slowly rose in the northern hemisphere, Pangol cried out: 'The Rebirth begins!'

At that moment the Doctor collapsed. He slumped against a pillar, his face grey and lined. He looked like a corpse. But incredibly he was still breathing.

9

Rebirth

Hardin found them in the Great Hall. Romana was trying to revive the Doctor.

'We must do something,' she whispered. 'I don't think he can stand another attack like this.'

Hardin had an idea. 'The laboratory. It's the only place we might be safe. Let's take him there.

'Help me,' she said.

Together they half carried the Doctor to the elevator. They left Pangol, who still sported the Helmet of Theron, trying to whip the Argolin into a burst of military enthusiasm. While there was no doubt that the old martial spirit was still present in many of the Argolin, increasing age had taken its toll. A high percentage of his forces would never make the battlefield.

While Romana did her best to revive the Doctor, Hardin set up the equipment in the laboratory.

'You know I've been thinking,' he said, 'what we need is a second Random Field Frame. The one we've got just isn't powerful enough to hold the field stable until we get proper cellular rejuvenation.'

'Where are we going to get a second Field Frame?' demanded Romana.

The Doctor suddenly roused himself. 'The TARDIS,' he said.

'What?'

'Use the Randomizer. It's easily adapted.'

Romana considered the problem for a moment.

Then decided against it: 'It's too risky.'

'It's my only chance.'

She knew it was true. He looked so old that she felt he would crumble to dust if she touched him.

Alone in the boardroom the ageing Mena watched on the video screens as Pangol strutted around the Great Recreation Hall. Wearing the Helmet he looked every inch the Argolin war leader.

'Guides of Argolis,' he proclaimed, 'according to our ancient laws, we, Pangol, are now your leader. We are the future. For what is about to happen, and for the aeons that lie ahead, I demand – as is my right – your unquestioning obedience...'

'I must stop this madness,' she muttered.

Mena rose unsteadily from her chair and took a few tottering steps towards the door. Her legs gave way under her and she fell to the floor.

The faint sound of the elevator door closing caused Romana and Hardin to look up from their deliberations. They realized the Doctor was no longer there. She ran to the elevator, knowing she would be too late.

'I'll go after him.'

'No. I think I know where he's gone.'

She switched the video screen in the laboratory through to the Great Hall. She cut from camera to camera, until she caught a fleeting glimpse of a familiar figure. She switched to a closer shot, and was rewarded by a sight of the Doctor shuffling towards the TARDIS.

'Oh, you fool! You crazy old fool!' she cried.

But of course the Doctor could not hear her.

Fortunately Pangol was in full flow. He had an attentive audience and had no intention of cutting short his peroration. His back was to the Doctor, who Romana saw disappear into the TARDIS.

'The termination of our honoured Chairwoman, our late Heresiarch, is now complete,' intoned the new Argolin leader. 'We shall remember her wise guidance, her sense of justice, her moderation – all virtues appropriate to a time of reconstruction. But that time is past...'

Hardin stared at the screen, unable to take in Pangol's words. 'What does he mean – Mena's termination? She can't be... surely she's not—'

Just as he left the laboratory she saw the Doctor again on the video screen. He was emerging from the TARDIS. He carried something underneath his arm. She saw that it was the Randomizer. He turned towards the camera for a moment, and she could have wept when she saw his face. It was the face of a tired old man who barely knew where he was. She could tell that he was on the verge of another attack. Only sheer will-power kept him going. He paused for a moment, then headed in the direction of the generator.

'No!' she cried when she realized his intention. 'Don't try and use the power of the generator! Bring the Randomizer here.'

The Doctor kept on going.

She wanted to look away. But it was like watching someone leap off a tall building. You knew you could not bear to witness the fall. Yet you stood, half-hypnotized, impelled to watch.

A Security guide entered and spoke to the self-appointed Heresiarch. The Foamasi shuttle was asking permission to take off. Pangol refused to give it.

'But, sir, they do have diplomatic priority,' said the guide.

'Not while I rule Argolis!'

The Doctor took advantage of the exchange to slip inside the generator.

As the door closed behind him, he seemed to lose his sense of purpose. For a long moment he looked round the black glass panels of the image chamber, trying to recall where he was. What am I doing here? he wondered. He frowned and closed his eyes, concentrating desperately on his mission. He had had a plan. But what was it?

'The anti-baryon shield,' he said at last. 'Yes, that was it. Wasn't it?'

His brain seemed to be composed of cotton wool. Where was the anti-baryon shield? His mind was blank.

He took out his sonic screwdriver and clumsily tried to remove one of the glass panels. But his gnarled fingers had no strength in them. At last he managed to loosen the magnetic catch on a panel. Yet still it would not come. He used both hands to prise it off – and lost his grip on the Randomizer. It fell to the floor and shattered into a dozen pieces.

The suns of Argolis had risen almost clear of the horizon when Romana reached the Great Hall. Pangol was holding out his arms to the suns as if welcoming their rays. She knew she did not have a moment to lose. There was no time to create a diversion: no time for any clever plan. She ran through the crowd in the Great Hall straight to the generator.

Two Security guides seized her before she could reach the door. She struggled in their arms, but it was useless. They were too strong.

'The Doctor's in there,' she pleaded. 'He's at his limit. He couldn't take any further ageing. It would kill him.'

'Good,' said Pangol. 'It will save him having to breathe the air of Argolis when we eject him from the Hive.'

Romana's protests were drowned by the voice of the Shuttle Launch Controller through the loudspeaker system. He announced that the Foamasi shuttle had taken off without permission.

'Destroy it,' ordered Pangol.

'But, sir, that is an act of war,' objected the Controller.

'Remember the Second Precept of Theron,' declared Pangol. ' "War is the right and duty of every Argolin." '

'Destroy the shuttle!'

As the suns rose – twin brilliant yellow objects – the whole sky was suddenly illumined by a burst of blinding white light. The sound of the explosion, though muffled by the glass of the dome, followed a moment later.

'Thus die the enemies of Argolis!' cried Pangol.

He settled the Helmet of Theron on his head and walked to the generator. He flung open the door and entered.

Romana struggled free from the Security guides. The Doctor was in the generator. Old and failing, he would stand no chance against the younger man. She flung herself at the door. But she was too late. The door closed in her face.

'Help me!' she called.

But no one moved.

She realized that they were staring up at the bubble screen.

In the bubble above the generator the helmeted image of Pangol appeared. The image grew larger. It swelled. Then, like cells dividing, the image separated into three. Three Pangols appeared where a second

118

before there had been only one. These images in their turn separated, each producing three perfect duplicates. The process was repeated over and over again. Serried ranks of Pangols formed in the bubble. The doors of the generator opened at last. The ranks of Pangols began to march out – all helmeted, all identical.

Romana stood appalled. She had a vision of what the New Argolis would be like. It would be an army consisting of millions upon millions of facsimiles, all obedient to one leader, all totally loyal to their one progenitor. It would be an army of Pangols. The older Argolin were dying out. Soon all that would be left would be a state populated by one man, multiplied a billion times. With the generator to reduplicate him endlessly, what was there to prevent him from fighting any war, regardless of losses? What was to prevent him from conquering other planets and populating them with himself? What was there to prevent Pangol from conquering the whole galaxy?

Jostled, forced backwards by the tide of helmeted figures, Romana tried to fight her way towards the generator.

'Remove this alien trash,' ordered the only begettor of the New Argolis. 'Let her breathe the air of Argolis.'

A number of helmeted figures seized her. Gloved hands muffled her screams. Struggling violently, she was lifted off her feet and carried towards the shuttle bay. She knew she would die on the surface of the planet.

Meanwhile the generator continued its sinister work. The sound of tramping feet filled the Great Recreation Hall.

Hardin had found Mena in the boardroom, where she

had collapsed. She was alone, having been deserted by all her Medical Guides who had joined Pangol. Her condition was grave. She was scarcely breathing at all, and when he took her pulse it was so weak he feared her heart had stopped beating.

He rolled up his jacket to make a pillow for her head. As he did so, he heard Pangol's voice come over the video screen: 'After you have disposed of the girl, get the body of the Chairwoman. That, too, must be left outside on the surface of the planet. We want no trace of past Heresiarchs here.'

They will not get Mena, thought Hardin. I'll see to that. She has perhaps one chance and one chance only...

He picked up the dying woman in his arms.

It was hopeless Romana knew. Struggle as she might, the helmeted figures were too strong for her. Then suddenly, as soon as they had carried her out of the Great Hall, she found herself being lowered to her feet. They let go of her.

Puzzled, she looked round the group of helmeted Pangols.

'What's going on?' she demanded.

One of the figures put his finger to his lips, signalling her to remain silent. He pushed back his helmet.

'Doctor!' she gasped.

For it was indeed the Doctor. No longer bent and white-haired, but youthful and rejuvenated. A mere seven hundred years old.

'Ssh,' said the Doctor.

Perhaps the effort of speaking proved too much for him — because he suddenly vanished into thin air! One minute he was grinning cheerfully at her from underneath his helmet, the next minute he was gone: disappeared.

The phenomenon, however, was not unique. In the Great Hall other members of Pangol's army were showing a distressing lack of substantiality. They tended to vanish quite suddenly, like snowflakes on a hotplate. There would be a squad of a hundred or so marching across the Hall. Then in the blink of an eye they would be reduced to ninety. A few steps later, fifty. Before they had gone twenty yards there would not be one left.

Another of the Argolin army removed his helmet to reveal a smiling Doctor.

'What's happening?' asked Romana.

The Doctor said: 'It's quite simple really. Tachyon images. Outwardly Pangol—'

Another soldier raised his helmet. It was a second Doctor.

'—inwardly me,' explained Doctor Number Two.

'Unfortunately,' observed a third Doctor, 'these tachyon images are basically unstable—'

But he, too, vanished before he could complete his sentence.

'Or fortunately,' remarked Doctor Number Two, 'depending on your point of view.'

And like the Cheshire Cat, he was gone.

'Doctor, which is you?' asked Romana.

'Here,' replied another of the soldiers. He took her arm. 'Come on. Back to the generator. We've got work to do.'

'Thank heavens,' she said. 'I was getting worried. At least you're solid.'

At which point the hand on her arm, and indeed the rest of the body attached to the hand, abruptly evaporated. Four, five, six other Doctors vanished one after another. In desperation Romana grabbed the last figure and clung to it.

'Careful,' protested the Doctor. 'I may be fragile.'

'Do you feel fragile?'

'I've got a bit of a headache and my feet hurt,' he complained. 'All in all, I have felt better.'

'But are you real?'

The Doctor poked himself in the chest with a cautious finger, an exercise which apparently did not fill him with confidence. 'Real-ish,' he ventured at last. 'That is to say, I seem to be all here. More or less. Give or take the odd molecule or two.

'I'd give me another moment or two, if I were you,' he advised. 'Maybe I need to set – like a jelly.'

Romana let go of him.

He did not vanish.

'Seems to be holding out,' he said at last. 'Wait a minute – I've lost my coat!'

'No time to bother about coats,' snapped Romana. 'We've got to do something for Mena.'

The Argolin guides watched their new leader in total silence. They were in a state of shock. Not surprisingly they were baffled by the turn of events. Within the space of only a few mintues they had witnessed the creation, and destruction, of a whole army – an act of military vandalism beyond the powers of even the most insane of Argolin generals.

Pangol had removed his helmet and stood at the data station console. He was running a checkout routine designed to test the computer programme. If necessary, he would patch the programme, thus overriding that part of it which had caused the trouble.

He refused to be disheartened by what he regarded as a mere hiccup, a minor technical hitch. The destruction of one army of doubles would not stop him. Once he had amended the programme and run a few tests, he would reset the controls of the generator. The rebirth of Argolis would begin again. A short delay was not important.

A figure pushed its way through the silent crowd of (real) Argolin. It was Hardin, carrying Mena in his arms. Ignoring Pangol he made his way to the generator.

It took the latter a moment before he realized what the Terran had in mind.

'Stop him!' he cried. 'The late Heresiarch is dead. That man must not be allowed to enter the generator with her dead body.'

Perhaps it was the shock of seeing Mena again, or perhaps it was at that moment that the old Argolin belief in absolute obedience to a leader died – at any rate no one moved to do Pangol's bidding. No one barred Hardin's way.

'I am in command!' shrilled Pangol.

'Mena's stopped breathing,' said the Terran simply. 'The generator is her only hope.'

'I am leader here! I order you to go back!'

Hardin shouldered Pangol aside. This sudden assault on his person galvanized the latter. All his resentment and disappointment came boiling to the surface. In a frenzy he flung himself on the Terran, whose arms were encumbered with the unconscious woman.

Almost with indifference the other Argolin watched as the two men wrestled at the door of the generator, each holding tight to the body of Mena. Then a fierce blow from Pangol sent Hardin sprawling to the floor. Triumphantly the young Argolin turned to face his people, with Mena in his arms. But the effort was too much for him. He lost his balance, staggered, and took a step backwards. He stepped over the threshold of the generator.

With a soft sigh the door closed automatically.

Pangol and Mena were trapped inside the generator.

Lights on the computer console flickered. Its programme was set in operation. There was a faint whine as power surged into the generator.

When the Doctor and Romana entered the Great Recreation Hall a moment later, they found Hardin struggling desperately to force open the door of the generator. Silent and unmoving the Argolin looked on.

'Look!' cried Romana. She pointed to the bubble screen.

There in the bubble they could see the images of Mena and Pangol. But the two images did not divide and reduplicate as they had done before. Instead they seemed to blend into each other.

'I set it up for rejuvenation, I think,' said the Doctor. 'But heaven knows what effect it will have.'

Romana shook her head. 'Anything could happen. The whole machine must have become totally unstable by now.'

Together they pulled on the doors of the generator with Hardin. But it was useless. Nothing would open them.

'The doors won't open while it's still running,' he gasped.

'Are you sure?' she said.

She went over to the data station console and started to try and abort the programme. But it was too late. When Pangol had reprogrammed the computer, he had written out the over-ride, which would have enabled anyone to stop or change the routine while it was running.

The Doctor picked up the Helmet of Theron which lay on the floor where it had fallen. He weighed it in his hand. The Helmet was heavy and made of a metal

124

hard enough to stop a missile from a bolt gun or blunt the edge of one of the great double-handed sabres used by the old Argolin in their frequent duels.

Adopting the stance of an Olympic shot-putter, the Doctor hurled the Helmet at the bubble screen.

There was a flash of light as the screen shattered into a thousand fragments. For a moment everyone was blinded. Then when sight returned, the Doctor saw the door of the generator slide open. A figure appeared in the doorway.

It was Mena.

But a younger Mena, slim and statuesque. She carried something in her arms.

A small baby, bawling like a wild thing.

Mena spoke: 'I think this child must be Pangol. I seem to recall that he looked very much like this when he was born.'

'Apparently the generator looks after its own,' observed Hardin.

The Doctor laughed. 'One thing about babies,' he said, 'is that they're pretty harmless. They can't cause wars or lead armies for a good twenty years.'

'Then the Argolin must bring up this one to be a man of peace.'

She handed the child to the Doctor to hold. He looked down at the angry, red, little creature with some alarm. Maybe I was wrong about babies, he thought. This one looks quite capable of anything.

But Mena had other things on her mind. 'First,' she said, 'we must contact the Foamasi and avert a war. Somehow we must make amends for the destruction of their shuttle.'

'Not necessary, madam, I assure you,' declared the familiar voice of Brock.

The Foamasi agent stalked through the crowd, his

lizard's tail swishing in what appeared to be a friendly manner.

'But I thought your shuttle—'

'One of my agents', replied the Foamasi, 'permitted the leader of the West Lodge, the creature who impersonated your accountant, to escape. Whether my man was merely inefficient or else in the pay of the criminal is something that only a full internal investigation by the Bureau will determine.

'In any case,' he continued, 'the question is academic. They took off together in our shuttle, which your Controller subsequently blew up. My congratulations. We are therefore in your debt.'

Mena wondered if she could capitalize on this indebtedness. After all one good turn deserves another. She knew that financing a new rejuvenation generator would require more capital than the Argolin possessed. She was already mentally planning the new publicity campaign: Come To Argolis And Grow Young.

While Mena and the Foamasi exchanged diplomatic compliments, the Doctor handed Hardin the baby.

'Here,' he said. 'Hold this.'

Romana was peering cautiously inside the door of the generator. 'We must get the Randomizer back,' she declared.

'Perhaps after we've run a checkout routine to see how much of the computer is still operational, it will be safe to go inside.'

But the Doctor had had enough of Randomizers to last him for a very long time. 'Why bother?' he said.

'We can't leave the Randomizer here.'

'Why not?'

'We'll never know where the TARDIS is going to turn up next.'

'Good,' replied the Doctor. 'Neither will the Black Guardian.

'Apart from Randomizers,' he went on, 'I'm getting sick and tired of bogeymen with ideas above their station. The cosmos is full of them.'

He walked over to the TARDIS and opened the door.

'There's been more than enough randomizing on this job.'

'This was supposed to be a holiday,' snapped Romana.

K9 still stood on the bench where they had left him. He was surrounded by a pool of seawater.

'Hello, K9,' said the Doctor. 'Pleased to see us?'

There was a strange whirring noise in the Great Recreation Hall. The Argolin looked round. They showed no particular surprise when the blue police box dematerialized. It had after all been one of those days.